# The 007 Dossier
## B.S. McReynolds

Illustrated by James Streeter

ISBN 0-9667203-7-7
**Book Publishing**
4034 Nobel Drive, #102
University City, CA 92122
Phone (619) 638-0669
Fax (619) 638-1828

Disclaimer: This book has been carefully and humorously written by the author, generously cartooned by the illustrator and respectfully presented by the publisher. Some of this book's text makes reference to specific passages from previously published works by other authors, and in each case herein the reference or quotation is carefully, thoroughly and immediately acknowledged and attributed within the adjacent text. The opinions expressed in this book are solely the author's; neither the author, illustrator nor publisher shall have any liability or responsibility to any person or entity with respect to any loss or damage caused, or alleged to be caused, either directly or indirectly by the opinions and publication of this book.

The 007 Dossier
ISBN 0-9667203-7-7
Copyright © 1999 by B.S. McReynolds

All rights reserved. No part of this book may be used or reproduced in any manner whatsoever without written permission from the author, except for the inclusion of attributed selections embodied in a literary review of this book. For review information or written permission, contact the publisher, BS Book Publishing, 4034 Nobel Drive, #102, University City, CA 92122, phone (619) 638-0669, fax (619) 638-1828

# *The 007 Dossier*
## B.S. McReynolds
Illustrated by James Streeter

ISBN 0-9667203-7-7

**BS Book Publishing**
4034 Nobel Drive, #102
University City, CA 92122
Phone (619) 638-0669
Fax (619) 638-1828

Other works by B.S. McReynolds, the author of
*The 007 Dossier,* include:
**Presidential Blips**
**Wild, Wild Women**

Author's acknowledgments:

I would like to thank Nancy Loper for her patience and typing. I also ask forgiveness for the misspelling of her name in my previous works. Thank you, Nancy.

I thank Patricia Miller Rains of Point Loma Publishing in San Diego for copyediting and typesetting this book.

Also, and not least, my thanks to Diana Lee for her nagging, pestering, badgering, demanding, fretting, vexing, insisting, urging, pressing, requiring, abusing, exhausting, imposing, baiting, stipulating, needling, black-mailing, scowling, intimidating, hinting, advising, monitoring and suggesting that I finish NOW.

## Contents

| | | |
|---|---|---|
| Introduction | page | 17 |
| Prologue | page | 11 |
| Chapter 1: The Creation | page | 15 |
| Chapter 2: Home And Comfort | page | 33 |
| Chapter 3: Bonded Habits | page | 39 |
| Chapter 4: Double 0 Seven = Gourmet? | page | 47 |
| Chapter 5: The Bond Girls | page | 53 |
| Chapter 6: Is This The One? | page | 61 |
| Chapter 7: Office Hanky Panky | page | 65 |
| Chapter 8: M & M's | page | 73 |
| Chapter 9: The Bond Mobiles | page | 81 |
| Chapter 10: Rogues, Scamps & No-Good-Nics | page | 91 |
| Chapter 11: The Swords Of St. Bond | page | 101 |
| Chapter 12: Chick Charts | page | 111 |
| Chapter 13: The Dirty Deed Doers | page | 147 |
| Chapter 14: The 007 Trivia Test | page | 163 |
| About The Author | page | 173 |
| Index | page | 175 |
| Ordering Coupon | page | 185 |

*The 007 Dossier*

***The 007 Dossier*** is dedicated to
    Lela "Bobby" Sutphen, my grandmother, and to Kathleen Mora Sutphen, my mother.

## Introduction

With all the hoop-la over Ian Fleming's magnificent creation *James Bond 007*, it is perhaps difficult to renounce the humble beginnings of that which he created. The first Bond books were seldom reviewed other than by Fleming's own employer, the *Sunday Times* of London. Even these reviews were less than raves. Particularly in the United States, the faddy fact of 007 was a long time in earning. The early hard-cover editions sold hardly 10,000 copies each.

Then by a stroke of the unexpected, John F. Kennedy released his list "My Ten Favorite Books" and low and behold Ian Fleming's *From Russia With Love* was in la-la land. At this time, the Bond books had been on the market nearly eight years since 1953 and had been read by an estimated 170,000 people. Several years later, at the time of Ian Fleming's death in 1964, nearly 40,000,000 copies of the Bond books had been sold and he had a guestimate of 165,000,000 readers. With the release of the newest James Bond book in 1998, *Zero Minus Ten* written by Raymond Benson, the fourth author in the series, nearly 370,000,000 books have been sold worldwide, translated into seventeen languages with an astounding 1,600,000,000 readers.

The total success of the James Bond character leads to an applicable question: Why is James Bond so popular? Only four other fictitious characters have achieved Ian

## The 007 Dossier

Fleming's remarkable worldwide success: Sherlock Holmes, Tarzan, Frankenstein and Dracula.

At first people didn't pay much attention to the guy. James Bond? Who was James Bond? What was a double O seven? He was just a modern-day Lone Ranger without a sidekick with little more appeal than perhaps Spider Man. But for some oddball reason, people kept reading the books and then flocking to the movie theaters to watch the movies, until 007 became bigger than life. No freelance gumshoe, Scotland Yard detective, hard-nosed New York cop or special agent has ever come across such a collection of no-good-nics, villains or rogues - as Bond encountered - not to mention the fact that every strumpet and tart he meets is ready to drop her drawers and share her favors with this fantasy.

Without too much difficulty at your favorite magazine rack, you can find many a novel of suspense and sex that would far surpass Ian Fleming's, Robert Markham's (Kingsley Amis), John Gardner's or Raymond Benson's gift to spin a yarn. In an article that Paul Johnson wrote entitled "Sex, Snobbery and Sadism" that appeared in the *New Statesman* he said, "I have just finished what is, without doubt, the nastiest book I have ever read." The book he had just finished reading was entitled *Dr. No*. Mr. Johnson continued to report that he would have stopped reading one-third of the way through if he were not convinced that it could be "a social phenomenon of some importance." Johnson went on to say that Ian Fleming "deliberately and systematically excites and then satisfies the worst instincts of ..." the reader.

Ian Fleming was most definitely obsessed with the idea of pain and sex; we read it on more than one occasion in his books. Apparently Robert Markham, John Gardner and Raymond Benson have carried on this attitude because we find similar scenes in their James Bond novels. In *Casino Royale*, Fleming says that while being tortured, 007 is

## Introduction

approaching "... a wonderful period of warmth and languor leading into a sort of sexual twilight where pain turned to pleasure and where hatred and fear of the torturers turned to a masochistic infatuation," (Chapter seventeen).

Any realistic approach by critic or fan to attack or praise with vim or vigor the writing of a novelist would be to make a valid expression concerning the style and quality of sex and violence and fiction contained within the writing. In *The 007 Dossier* no analysis of the 20th century's most popular fantasy figure is intended; only a review of the substructure and characters, and the presentation of a logical, dialectical and poignant past for 007. It is not the intent of this book to pin down James Bond and dissect him like one would a bug but perhaps only to place him on a glass slide and look closely at him through a microscope FOR FUN. **B.S. McReynolds**

The Kennedy family, particularly United States President John F. Kennedy and Mrs. Jacqueline Kennedy, introduced CIA Director Allen Dulles to the works of Ian Fleming with a copy of *From Russia With Love*. Mrs. Kennedy said, "Here is the book you should read, Mr. Director."          ... as told by **Allen Dulles**

*The 007 Dossier*

*Prologue*

Before proceeding into the individual details of 007's life and the application of his being, it is important to put both of these items into a most appropriate frame of accountable reference, in order to make this literary champion into the true sense of a mock-person. James Bond could easily be said to exemplify an important microcosm of real life – all of the innovative and anachronistic secret agents of his era. His originality was so well designed, it became typical and thus copied to excess by the scores of fictional mock secret agents of the latter part of the 20th century, so much so that one is continually tempted to draw and compare general conclusions from his individual assignments, skills and depth of carnal knowledge.

Double 0 seven, this mock-person, was so independent and believable to some readers that at times he was labeled a far-right terrorist, so intransigent was he in his dedication to his task that any other unrelated activity seemed a compromise. He demonstrated complete confident of his future, or of even surviving to have a future. At moments of his greatest stress, he was so discreet, scrupulous and guarded that he could shepherd and balance several delightful chicks – even though to his readers his future seemed at best NOT CERTAIN. Yet he was still able to, in his own mind, logically reconcile all these on-going contradictions without relinquishing any part of his own great honesty and profound sense of humanity, even controlling those raging-bull hormones within himself until the proper time of their release.

By Jove, you have to admire a man with these traits.

If one were to credit two elements above all for consideration of James Bond's wellspring, the first would have to be the man himself, the second would have to be in the manner that he carried out his artistry, that being a secret agent. However, some would say his artistry was his knowledge of being able to remove cobwebs for females. Say what?

Consequently, the many years during which he was able to observe – and in the numerous occasions when he passionately participated in – the diverse political ideas and movements of the second half of the 20th century were quite useful to him. From the aftermath of the romanticism of World War II, to the revolutionary events and half victories of the Eastern world, to the transparent excesses of the Western world, Bond had the opportunity to familiarize himself with these struggles and to act upon them and counteract them with a sophisticated maturity, at least as far as his believers and followers were concerned, which was not possible for the great number of other fictional mock-secret-service agents who followed him to the book-peddlers.

So there it is!

Any other element essential to our professed understanding of this mock person consists entirely of his boundless enthusiasm, his good will and his insatiable curiosity about any experience which might enrich the techniques of the craft he pursued. He basically kept an open, alert mind for any suggestion which might, in his opinion, show him a better way to serve King/Queen and Country and to avoid getting into an ever fearful rut. The enduring quality of his forte stems from his continuing

## *Prologue*

independence from any routine established by himself or his colleagues. It resulted in changes of well thought out plans, to techniques which occasionally seem to more than suggest a certain instability and often discontent peers and rivals, who would relish to discover a weakness in those characteristics of which they grew accustomed to rely on – be they pro or con, logical or ridiculous.

Although it would be unjust to state, as some critics have done, that 007 was too easily influenced, the close-truth is that he always regarded sympathetically the innovations of peers and foes in their endeavors. Double 0 seven possessed the conscious modesty of an artisan who, observing both tried and true and new and bold techniques, would in a moment determine which would best solve his situation and utilize it to enrich his life and answer the problem facing him.

These goals, aims, quests, ambitions – as we can see them in another aspect of Fleming's constant concern – were always, as is now, to portray evil as evil as sensitively as possible, to capture its fundamental and eternal quality for what it signified. For Bond, the reality of St. George and the Dragon lay in its close intimacy with his being, hence the appeal to his followers and numerous well-wishers.

Of all the secret agents, James Bond, 007 is the single character who has most strongly emphasized the presence of good and evil in people, in his assignments, in his conclusions. The mock secret agents have nearly always treated these subjects independently and aside from the point. At any given time, only 007 brings into harmony all the elements of an '*affaire de coeur*.' There is total accord between good and evil, right and wrong, St. George and the Dragon or hero and heroine. Because of this, following his exploits, many readers have found a certain intimacy, a certain kinship with 007. One is frequently tempted to read a sort of symbolism and moralism into the presentation of his assignments. James Bond's adventures were base

## The 007 Dossier

prototypes; almost archetypes for the mock secret agents to follow for various wordsmiths.

There is nothing of the sort in Ian Fleming's work. If one observed the truth with fidelity equal to that of the creator, one would find his liking for commonplace and orderly things. He didn't take aim at anything moral or push undercurrents of social philosophy, which in reality does not mean that he was indifferent, only mindful not to create tidal waves. Less widely noted, Fleming had no desire to deliver either a spiritual or political message with his typewriter, although in his experimental efforts he did seek originality for his creation for its own sake, a hallmark of distinctiveness. Yet he was unorthodox when it suited his graphic needs, even at the risk of appearing inconsistent by abandoning techniques which he had found most useful. The stages of his creation are invariably earmarked by the use of a 'modus operandi' suited for each perception.

In his period of labor, Fleming became convinced of the virtues of a division of created atmosphere, with a subtle humanosity. Although he might support just criticism, he was never blindly submissive to its demands. All of Fleming's work represents an intimate union between creator and creation, his concept of fictional reality and his emotions as a writer, reflecting a sincere and unaffected yarn for fun, supported by a knowledgeable technique, which in no way reduced the initial impact of what he created. This most impressive achievement maintained a freshness and style of a Van Gogh - and is what gave the art of Fleming a brilliance and spontaneity to endure for generations and perhaps for eons. It both characterizes and justifies the long lasting relations of the followers for every step, curve and turn he had taken. Just for fun.

## Chapter 1: The Creation

Ian Fleming's fantastic phenomenon began in January of 1952 on the island of Jamaica at his retreat home near Orasabcssa in the three-bedroom home which Fleming had had built - and named *GoldenEye* for one of two reasons. The first reason was that *GoldenEye* had been a code name for a wartime operation conceived and led by Fleming when he was in Naval Intelligence. The second reason was that a novel written by an American author named Carson McClullen, *Reflections In a Goldeneye,* was one of his favorites.

For whatever motive, Fleming needed an attention-getter to remove his thoughts from his quickly approaching future. That being, "the shock of getting married at forty-three." His mind was more than likely on a number of matters but the matter that was first and foremost on his mind was his impending marriage to Anne Rothermere, whose divorce from Lord Rothermere was to be announced on February 8th. It was Anne who recommended that perhaps he could amuse himself and write something. This might have jolted his memory to a time just before his release from his wartime duty. A friend had asked Fleming what he would do when a civilian again, and his reply was "to write the spy story to end all spy stories."

Pondering what to name his adventurous vision, knowing only that he wanted "the dullest name he could

15

## The 007 Dossier

find," Fleming discovered it on his own coffee table, on a book which was one of his favorites, *Birds of the West Indies*, written by an ornithologist named James Bond. Fleming promptly christened his literary hero James Bond and began the novel that would make him famous beyond his wildest dreams.

*{To the left is a revised and more finished version of Bond's coat of arms that was designed by the Rouge Dragon. The College of Arms solicited by Ian Flaming, for On Her Majesty's Secret Service in 1963.}*

When first we meet Commander James Bond, Royal Naval Volunteer Reserve (R.N.V.R.). (Just what, where or who he commanded we are not informed.) In *Casino Royale*, we are told that he had been employed by the British Secret Service (MI-6) since 1938 or 1939. But then, according to chapter twenty-one entitled *Orbit* of *You Only Live Twice*, he was still in his teens and attending school at this time. Even with these conflicting stories, he is 007 "The senior of the three men in the Service who have earned the Double 0 number" which gives them the right to kill. (Think about that for a moment. The license to kill. That's HEAVY!)

In *Casino Royale*, chapter eight, Bond tells a friend, "It's not difficult to get a Double 0 number if you're

## Chapter 1: The Creation

prepared to kill people," he said. "That's all the meaning it has. It's nothing to be particularly proud of."

What does the "double O" status mean to you and me? It would do no good to romanticize that Commander James Bond is not a most highly trained professional killer. He has killed as a soldier, he has killed for a friend (M), he has killed in a vendetta, he has killed in self-defense, he has killed in a test, he has killed in cold blood and he has killed for King/Queen and country. His exploits have most faithfully been set to paper for nearly 50 years, and actually we have learned a great deal about James Bond. He is a highly valued servant of the King/Queen's government and very valuable to have around when one is in a Sticky-Wickett (especially if you happen to be young and pretty and have square-cut fingernails). Double Os are not passed out at random; they must be earned in a way that would make most people throw up.

The following is an account of the justified killing that served to earn James Bond his Double O classification, his official license to kill. His most coveted OO rating. His Ling Ling Chat (007 in Cantonese, which is told to us by T.Y. Loo in *Zero Minus Ten*, chapter five).

"The first was in New York - a Japanese cipher expert cracking our codes on the thirty-sixth floor of the RCA building in Rockefeller Center. I took a room on the

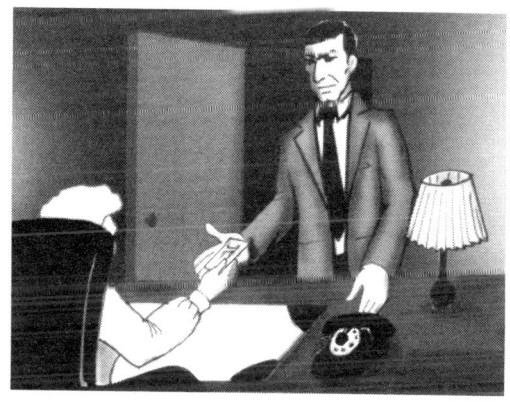

17

## *The 007 Dossier*

fortieth floor of the next door skyscraper, and I could look across the street into his room and see him working. Then I got a colleague from our organization in New York, and a couple of Remington thirty thirty's with telescopic sights and silences. We smuggled them up to my room and sat for days waiting for our chance. He shot at the man a second before me. His job was only to blast a hole through the window so that I could shoot the Jap through it. They have tough windows at Rockefeller Center to keep the noise out. It worked very well. As I suspected, his bullet got deflected by the glass window and went God knows where. But I shot immediately after him, through the hole he had made. I got the Jap in the mouth as he turned to gape at the broken window."

"Bond smoked for a minute."

"It was a pretty sound job. Nice and clean too. Three hundred yards away. No personal contact. The next time in Stockholm wasn't so pretty. I had to kill a Norwegian who was doubling against us for the Germans. He'd managed

to get two of our men captured - probably bumped off for all I know. For various reasons it had to be an absolutely silent job. I chose the bedroom of his flat and a knife. And, well, he just didn't die very quickly."

"For those two jobs I was awarded a Double 0 number in the Service. A Double 0 in our Service means you've had to kill a chap in cold blood in the course of some job," (*Casino Royale*, chapter twenty).

Wow-wee! Perhaps you should read that last paragraph again.

If any other thriller writer had written a passage such

## Chapter 1: The Creation

as this, it would have been put down as pure straightforward invention. But Ian Fleming was no ordinary writer of fiction, and the foregoing just could have been a lethal insight into the secret life of Fleming.

Basically lone wolves, the 00s seem to be a curious lot. What? Sexual rivalry is the closest they seem to get in camaraderie - 007 vs. 006 - with Mary Goodnight the prize. They tend to show no interest in each other as individuals, but this may be one of the qualifications for entrance to the most envied section of the Service. Double 0 seven is probably better off this way; he tends to socialize with Bill Tanner, M's Chief of Staff, with the occasional lunch or golf game and then perhaps, the once-a-year binge with another of the Double 0 boys, after the completion of a tough assignment. NOT!

Male bonding does not seem to be in Bond's bag. Double 0 seven is most definitely a ladies' man, rather than a man's man. Bond's idea of a good time is -

19

## The 007 Dossier

conceivably, to poke fun at a girl.
Well, why not? It's better than shooting rabbits.
Double 0 seven? What is 007? Is he a modern day Peruses, armed by Q Branch to slay Medusa? Maybe, a St. George in an Aston-Martin DBIII in a high speed chase

to kill the dragon? How about a Don Quixote in search of the windmill of M's mind? None of these exactly, but a 20th Century figure of modern idiom, perhaps uniquely equipped to deal with the problems of his world. Commander James Bond cannot be known as a hero. This would blow his cover. And he cannot be labeled a spy. This would be most inaccurate, for the dictionary defines spy as, "One employed to obtain secret information of military affairs of other countries." Now, 007's only true secret stealing adventure came in *From Russia With Love* when, with the help of Tatianna Romanova, he acquired a Soviet cipher machine - and then Bond acted only as a courier.

In the true sense of the word, Ian Fleming was a SPY, a label of paid, government-employed killer; or perhaps anti-spy or secret agent would be appropriate for 007. The fact that James Bond was decorated with the C.M.G. (Companion to the Order of St. Michael and St. George) in 1954, an award usually given only upon

## Chapter 1: The Creation

retirement from the Secret Service, is more than a measure of his value.

So it's Commander James Bond C.M.G., R.N.V.R. He is entitled to append the initials C.M.G. but 007, not being vain about that sort, most likely never will.

Fleming said of 007 in conversation, "Bond is not a hero, nor is he depicted as being very likable or admirable. He is a Secret Service Agent. He's not a bad man, but he is ruthless and self-indulgent. He enjoys the fight - he also enjoys the prize. In fiction, people used to have blood in their veins. Nowadays they have pond water. My books are just out of step. But then so are all the people who read them."

To the 007 fan, he is a tough Secret Service Agent who serves King/Queen and country and gets hurt and hospitalized - and girls, girls, girls while doing his duty.

James Bond, the Secret Service Agent, tends to be very secretive about his early years. One of the earliest tidbits is recorded in *From A View To A Kill* when we are informed that in "Paris at the age of sixteen," James Bond had, "...one of the most memorable evenings of his life, culminating in the loss, almost simultaneously, of his virginity and his notecase." From there he must have gone straight to Switzerland, because in *Role of Honor*, chapter eighteen, we discover that "...he'd been sixteen the first time he had visited Lake Geneva. He had spent a week with friends in Montreux, had a small affair with a waitress from a lakeside cafe and developed a taste for Campari-soda, (*Once*

21

## The 007 Dossier

Learned, Twice Tried). (I think it would be safe to say "He Liked It.")

Apparently, during his first visit to the Continent, he spent some time at the chalet of Hannes Oberhauser, because Bond tells us in *Octopussy* that "He taught me to ski before the war when I was in my teens. He was a wonderful man. He was something of a father to me at a time when I happened to need one."

Although the authors of the Bond adventures have not gotten around to informing us of many more details - either singly or combined, these pieces of information would, could and should make an interesting story of a restless young James Bond pre-007.

In none of the stories are we enlightened as to whether 007 ever did correct his age with M or the Secret Service. But for the present, what we wish to do is establish an age and a background for our subject.

## Chapter 1: The Creation

In an open letter published in 1964 in *The Times* quoted in *You Only Live Twice*, chapter twenty-one, after 007 was believed killed in Japan while disposing of Blofeld, M gives us the following information concerning Bond's early years and how he comes to be a Secret Service Agent:

"James Bond was born of a Scottish father, Andrew Bond of Glencoe and a Swiss mother, Monique Delacroix, from the Canton de Vaud. His father being a foreign representative of the Vickers armaments firm, his early education, from which he inherited a first-class command of French and German, was entirely abroad. When he was eleven years of age, both his parents were killed in a climbing accident in the Aquilles Rouges above Chamonix, and the youth came under the guardianship of an aunt, since deceased, Miss Charmain Bond, and went to live with her at the quaintly named hamlet of Pett Bottom near Canterbury in Kent. There, in a small cottage hard by the attractive Duck Inn, his aunt, who must have been a most erudite and accomplished lady, completed his education in an English public school, and at the age of twelve or thereabouts, he passed satisfactorily into Eaton, for which college he had been entered at birth by his father. It must be admitted that his career at Eaton was brief and undistinguished, and after only two halves, as a result, it pains me to record, of some alleged trouble with one of the boy's maids, his aunt was requested to remove him. She managed to obtain his transfer to Fettes, his father's old school. Here the atmosphere was somewhat Calvinistic and both academic and athletic standards were rigorous.

Nevertheless, though inclined to be solitary by nature, he established some firm friendships among the traditionally famous athletic circles at the school. By the time he left, at the early age of seventeen, he had twice fought for the school as a lightweight and had, in addition, founded the first serious judo class at an English public school. By now it was 1941, and by claiming an age of

23

## The 007 Dossier

nineteen and with the help of an old Vickers colleague of his father, he entered a branch of what was subsequently to become the Ministry of Defense. To serve the confidential nature of his duties, he was accorded the rank of lieutenant in the special branch of the R.N.V.R., and it is a measure of the satisfaction his services gave to his superiors that he ended the war with the rank of commander. It was about this time that the writer became associated with certain aspects of the ministry's work and it was with much gratification that I accepted Commander Bond's postwar application to continue working for the ministry in which, at the time of his lamented disappearance, he had risen to the rank of Principal Officer in the Civil Service."

This information does not reveal Bond's age but we learn in *Moonraker*, written in 1955, that he was in his middle thirties. So, by backtracking from there and estimating that before World War II, when he added a few years to his age, he was 16 or 17. That would have been 1941. At the end of the war in 1945, James Bond would have been 21, giving him a birth year of 1924. (However, in 1973 John Pearson wrote *James Bond - The Authorized Biography of 007* in which he selected a birthdate of November 11, 1920, which was Armistice Day.) Meanwhile, there is no evidence proving or disproving this in any of the writings of the Bond adventures by Ian Fleming, Robert Markham, John Gardner or Raymond Benson. So *The 007 Dossier* will use the date of November 11, 1920, as the official birthdate of James Bond, seeing as it was authorized by the subject in John Pearson's book.

If you use any other date, things would start to get

## Chapter 1: The Creation

really confusing. Nineteen twenty, 1924 and 1933 are all suggested as birth years for Bond. But really, considering all the time 007 has spent in clubs, casinos, bars and strolling along the beach, it is surprising that not one of his female friends has asked him directly - or at least asked his astrological sign. This could, should and would have pinpointed his beginning. But alas, this wasn't to be. Taking all things into consideration, things could start to get SUPER confusing if you used any birth year other than 1920.

In 1955, we are informed that at the age of 45, which should be approximately 1965, James Bond was going to be forcibly retired from the Double O Section because of

## The 007 Dossier

his age. If you used any date other than 1920, James Bond would have been a young shaver when he purchased his first Bentley in 1933. This would have been a nice set of wheels to cruise chicks at the age of nine - if Bond had been born in 1924.

And then also in *Casino Royale*, when 007 won 40 million francs on the flip of a card from Le Chiffre. This would have been nice spending money for a Scottish lad in a toyshop.

If Bond had retired in 1965, would he have retired to a chain of crumpet shops or to a fish and chip place with a Super Super Secret Secret recipe?

(Thinking about it. James Bond, if he were born in 1920, would be one year older than John Glenn when he returned to space in 1998. So why shouldn't 007 at whatever his age not chase and claim at least three chicks per book? It's possible!) What? But in actuality, James Bond, 007 doesn't and most likely never will have a given birthdate, birth year or birthday. He is ageless and will remain as such. (Maybe.) He is never going to age. Time doesn't move on. Kind of like Mickey Mouse, Bugs Bunny, Superman and that bunch. No candle added each year to some dumb cake. No, No Way Jose, we can't have James Bond, 007 in the year 2110 being 190 years old. No way can we have 007 with a walker pursuing no-good-nics or femme fatales with that type of transportation. It just wouldn't fly. So anything mentioned as a birthdate or a year of birth in *The 007 Dossier* is just pretend. Here, try this on, taste this, not real, meaningless. It ain't going to happen. It's just for fun.

There, that should clear that up.

With NO age placed on Bond, be it confusing as it may, let us proceed to a description. Readers of the Bond books have been told more than once that 007's appearance was similar to a young Hoggy Carmichael's. To the younger generation, most likely the face of Barry Nelson, Sean Connery, David Niven, George Lazenby,

## Chapter 1: The Creation

Roger Moore, Timothy Dalton or Pierce Brosnan has been substituted. This could leave you dazzled, befuddled, flustered or muddled but whenever I read Bond, I always put the face of Fleming to Bond - be the author Fleming, Markham, Gardner or Benson. I watch the movies enjoying the talents of Nelson, Connery, Niven, Lazenby, Moore, Dalton and Brosnan.

In reading the books more than a few times, we are told that the scar on Bond's face was on his right cheek (this being the right cheek of his face). Once in *The Spy Who Loved Me*, the scar was somehow placed on the left. But this may be because Vivienne Michel got oh sooo confused after that very hot and steamy shower Yea.

SMERSH, the Russian anti-spy organization, had a pretty bulky dossier gathered on James Bond, 007 (*From Russia With Love*) and we are most fortunate and privileged to be granted a peep into it:

"First name: James; Height 183 centimeters; Weight: 76 kilograms; slim build; Eyes: blue; Hair; black; scar down right cheek and on left shoulder; signs of plastic surgery on back of right hand; all around athlete; expert pistol shot, boxer, knife-thrower, does not use disguises. Language: French and German. Smokes heavily (N.B. special cigarettes with three gold bands) vice: drink, but not to excess, and women. Not thought to accept bribes."

A full page is skipped, which the reader tends to resent, and then we are informed that: "This man is invariably armed with a .25 Beretta automatic carried in a holster under his left arm. Magazine holds eight rounds. Has been known to carry a knife strapped to his left forearm; has used steel-capped shoes; knows the basic holds of judo. In general fights with tenacity and has high tolerance of pain."

The report is concluded:

"This man is a dangerous professional terrorist and spy, he has worked for the British Secret Service since

## The 007 Dossier

1938." If you backtracked using the year 1938, keeping in mind that at the age of 17, James Bond added a few years to his age to join up in the time of his country's need, a birth year of 1921 would be the result.

But in reading *You Only Live Twice*, we are told that the year was 1941.: "The Double 0 number signifies an agent who has killed and is privileged to kill on active service.

## Chapter 1: The Creation

There are believed to be only two other British agents with this authority. The fact that this spy was decorated with the C.M.G. in 1954, an award usually given only on retirement from the Secret Service, is a measure of his worth. If encountered in the field, the fact and full detail to be reported to headquarters."

Several photographs of James Bond were also in the possession of SMERSH. The best is a copy of an enlarged passport photo. "It was a dark lean-cut face, with a three- inch scar showing whitely down the sunburned skin of the right cheek. The eyes are wide and level under straight, rather long black brows. The hair is black, parted on the left, and carelessly brushed so that a thick black comma fell down over the right eyebrow. The longish straight nose ran down to a short upper lip below which was a wide and finely drawn but cruel mouth. The line of the jaw is straight and firm. A section of dark suit, white shirt and black knitted tie completed the picture," (*From Russia With Love*, chapter six).

The maturing 007 is seen through the eyes of Miss Moneypenny as she fantasizes about Bond in her office, in the 1981 release of John Gardner's *License Renewed*, chapter two: "She stared into space for a moment, her head filled with the afterimage of the man who had just entered M's inner sanctum: the bronzed good-looking face with rather long dark eyebrows above the wide, level blue eyes; the three inch scar which just showed down his right cheek; the long, very straight nose and the fine, though cruel mouth. Minute flecks of gray had just started to show in the black hair that still retained its boyish black comma about the right eye. As yet, no plumpness had appeared around the jowls and the line of the jaw was as straight and firm as ever. It was the face of an attractive buccaneer."

Apparently 007 has stood up remarkably well over the years. In 1981, when the foregoing was written, the man could be any age between 48 and 60, with a birth year

## *The 007 Dossier*

of from 1920 to 1933. Bond would have a pretend age from 52 to 64 in 1984 when *Role of Honor* was written. During that adventure, 007 carried off to bed no less than three conquests and caught the eye of several others. With the release of *The Man From Barbarossa* in 1991, Bond showed no signs of slowing down. At this time he could have been somewhere between 59 and 71 (pretending) years old.

If he keeps this pace, he's going to die, perhaps with a big smile on his face, but it's inevitable that he is going to die. This is not just an assumption, it was documented in four of Fleming's books. Each of the incidents described how 007 would have to breathe deeply to quiet his pounding heart.

When it comes to female conquests, 007 is the perpetual, standing "erect" cad. In the 1980s and 1990s, this may not be very admirable but apparently it is most acceptable. Perhaps, during the 13-year coma, Q-Branch might have fitted him with a super-duper pacemaker. Of

## Chapter 1: The Creation

course now there's the most wondrous drug of Viagra, so 007 should be going strong into the year 2020 and well beyond. That's cool. Even with all Bond's sexual conquests, we never heard him ask, "Did mine win?" We just assumed it didn't?

*The 007 Dossier*

## Chapter 2: Home And Comfort

Double 0 seven most assuredly has ironclad, nearly immovable viewpoints as to his likes and dislikes. Of the Double O boys, Bond is arguably the most stylized of the lot. We read of Sea-Island cotton shirts, tropical worsted trousers, dark blue alpaca suits - serge is also acceptable, depending on the climate, dark blue socks, black moccasin slip-on shoes (never shoelaces). "Shoelaces break at the damnedest times," (*Zero Minus Ten*, chapter four). Also thin black knitted ties worn with a regular round-over-and-through knot, never a Windsor knot - as those seem to be for the no-good-nics) and heavy white silk shirts. Golfing in Sea-Island shirts of dark-blue, wearing black casual shoes or sandals with a windcheater and slacks of hound-tooth.

Underclothes of nylon or Sea-Island-Cotton, and, for beach wear, white linen trunks, dark blue leather sandals. For a top, the dark blue silk pajama shirt, which is from Hong Kong, or a Japanese kimono - and then of course the inevitable single-breasted white dinner jacket worn with a black satin tie accented by a Rolex Oyster Perpetual

## The 007 Dossier

Chronometer with an expanding metal bracelet (which can also be used as a most effective knuckle-buster).

Of course 007 believes in a man's shave, using a Gillette of the old fashioned design, the heavy-toothed type. His luggage is battered pigskin, but at one time it was expensive.

In *The Facts Of Death*, chapter three, we were told, "The entire roomful of people couldn't help but notice James Bond, a splendid figure of a man dressed in a black three-piece single breasted Brioni dinner suit with peaked lapels and no vents. He wore a deep bow tie, and the tucked in white silk pocket handkerchief made the picture complete." To crown this picture of suaveness, 007 got himself a vodka and surveyed the guests. "Three women of various ages were eyeing him..." So, there it is - of course, you and me, being most assuredly lesser mortals, are not only envious, jealous, in awe, stupefied, impressed, wonder-struck at the total perfection of this wondrous being, we are also going to be in competition and are mad. No way are we going home with companionship. He's won and hasn't spoken a word.

Accordingly, I believe that we will find a little more than a minimum of vanity in Bond, but then a maximum of comfort may play a large part in his selection of a wardrobe, because his style of dress hasn't changed that much over the course of the years.

Bond's compromise in wearing only the pajama top is just a little unbelievable. Men may wear only the pajama bottoms and not the top, but never the top and no bottoms. A woman can answer the door in a pajama top only and not much is thought about it; let her answer in pajama bottoms alone and things may get a little out of hand. Now reverse that. If a man answers the door in pajama bottoms,

## Chapter 2: Home And Comfort

everything is kosher. Let him answer the same door in only a pajama top and he might find himself in front of a judge.

Then of course there's May, Bond's treasured yet elderly Scottish housekeeper, to contend with. And it is not likely that she is going to put up with much of his tomfoolery. May is from the old school and seems very straight.

She serves Bond his coffee from silver service by Queen Anne, his meals on Minton china of a special dark-blue with white and gold accents, and his morning egg in that super special dark-blue egg cup with a gold ring around the top.

And really, what of May? I'm quite certain she would never take orders from a long-legged, leggy, sunburned femme fatale with proud-perky-luscious breasts with pink nipples like wild raspberries, a derriere like a boy's, with square-cut fingernails and a sensual mouth, hair falling heavily to the nape of her sexy neck. A Tiffany-type in the kitchen would most likely make a cute picture, especially in an ornate evening gown that reveals the "deep valley between her breasts," but the real question would be,

35

## The 007 Dossier

could she get something stewing besides 007's blood?

The real topic here is where does Bond keep his stuff? Apparently, 007 keeps a comfortable flat located in the plane tree-lined stylish neighborhood of Chelsea on, of course, the ground floor for easy access and escape for when things might get SCARY. It's a converted Regency house off a small square near Kings Road. The particular square is not identified but could, with further research, be placed within several hundred yards. But it wouldn't be cricket to advertise that information.

Bond lives there alone with the exception of May, who is devoted to him. She knows that 007's work is of a dangerous nature, but she must suffer the agonies of her curiosity for she is far too dedicated to attempt to find out about his very secretive life.

It's a flat of limited space; sitting room, three bedrooms and kitchen. For 007 it's convenience; only a

## Chapter 2: **Home And Comfort**

mere 10 minutes' driving time to the MI-6 headquarters. The sitting room with its book-lined wall is decorated with an ornate Empire desk where he does his studying, mostly manuals with technical jargon, and practices the art of the fast card shuffle. Bond's bedroom is "smallish" and decorated with deep-red curtains and "Cole" wallpaper of white and gold. There seem to be two phones in the flat on the desk, one a standard phone and, of course, the red one with a direct hook-up to headquarters - which rings at the most inappropriate times.

Being that Bond's flat is most smallish as the others in the area and that May lives there full time, 007 must do his wenching elsewhere.

So in 1981, we learn of "his recently and newly decorated country cottage." In *License Renewed*, chapter two, we read that "...this was to be his first free weekend at the cottage." But duty had called and Bond had to postpone his plans with an "...agile, superbly nubile blonde." 007 had known her on and off for years and "...the fact that she lived only six miles from the cottage had greatly influenced Bond's purchase."

How long Bond kept the cottage we are not informed. In 1997, in *Zero Minus Ten*, chapter one, we learn that 007 had a new retreat home away from London. He "had purchased the property a year ago. Even though the heyday of a British Jamaica was long gone. Bond had always loved the island. For years, the memories and dreams he had of Jamaica haunted him. He had a compelling desire to be there. When a well-known British journalist and author died, the property became available, and Bond bought it. Thus, in addition to his flat in London, he now owned a secluded holiday home on his favorite island. Since buying it, Bond

## The 007 Dossier

had spent all of his available free time between missions at the sparsely furnished house. He called it "Shamelady" after a plant that grows wild along Jamaica's north shore, a sensitive plant that curls up if touched."

Now Bond, at the guesstimated age unknown, could do his wenching some 3,000 miles from home. Far, far, far out of the sight of May, his much trusted cook, housekeeper and alarm clock.

## Chapter 3: **Bonded Habits**

Double 0 seven's success as a fantasy figure comes mostly from his creator's knack for giving him decisive likes and dislikes, making him a person. Bond loves women, cars, guns, his job and of course a fine meal. After each meal, not to mention party time on a sofa, bed, floor or the beach, he enjoys his cigarette. Double 0 seven smokes enough to be declared a "smog zone." He goes through some 60 cigarettes a day. In one book, *Casino Royale*, he smoked as many as 70 cigarettes a day!

39

## The 007 Dossier

These were the Virginian blend of Balkan and Turkish tobacco, which were mixed and made for him by Morland's of Grosvenor Street. These custom cigarettes were wrapped in a special paper with three gold rings and had a higher content of nicotine than would be available for the average Joe Schmoe.

Bond's custom-made, hand-made, special-made cigarettes are carried in a gunmetal case that holds 50. They are lit with an oxidized Dunhill/Ronson cigarette lighter. In *The Man With The Golden Gun* Bond tried, on orders from his doctor, to cut back to 20 a day. But apparently this was impossible, because in 1981 Bond had arranged with "Morelands (notice the spelling change) of Grosvenor for a new special blend of cigarettes with a tar content slightly lower than any currently available on the market." (*License To Kill*, chapter two) Now nearly 50 years later, he is still using the same cigarette lighter and the same cigarette case.

Again in the '80s, Bond changed his smoking habits, as he: "...quietly lit one of his special low-tar cigarettes, originally made for him by Morland/Moreland's of Grosvenor Street and now produced - after much discussion and bending of rules - by H. Simmons of Burlington Arcade: the earliest known cigarette manufacturer in London. This firm even agreed to retain the distinctive three gold rings together with their own silhouette trademark on each of the specially produced cigarettes, and Bond felt not a little honored that he was the only customer who could coax personalized cigarettes from Simmons." (*For Special Services*, chapter four)

Figuring Bond smoked 60 cigarettes a day for a period of nearly 50 years with the occasional light for the

## Chapter 3: **Bonded Habits**

ladies, he has used that same lighter close to 1,200,000 times. Estimating a count of 20 cigarettes per pack at a cost of $2.00 per pack, he has spent $120,000 on 60,000 packs!

The facts of Bond's bad habits have been documented for nearly 50 years, including the pleasure he finds in alcohol. Double 0 seven is never pie-eyed on the job. However, on occasion, he pretends to be, especially when he's playing cards with millionaire no-good-nics to encourage them to be overly confident. Between assignments it may be another matter, as we learn from his medical report: "when not engaged upon strenuous duty, the officer's average daily consumption of alcohol is in the range of half a bottle of spirits of between sixty and seventy proof. On examination, there continues to be little definite sign of deterioration. The tongue is furred. The blood pressure is a little raised at 160/90. The liver is not palpable, on the other hand, when pressed the officer admits to frequent occipital headaches and there is spasm in the Trapeziums muscles and so-called "Filrosite" modules can be felt. I believe these symptoms to be due to the officer's mode of life. He is not responsive to the suggestion that over-indulgence is no remedy for the tensions in his professional calling and can only result in the creation of a toxic state which could finally have the effect of reducing his fitness as an officer," (*Thunderball*, chapter one).

In addition to the occasional bottle of Don Perignon, the select glass of wine and bottle of beer, Bond enjoys bourbon on the rocks. He seems to favor Old Grand Dad, Jack Daniels, I.W. Harpers and Walker's Deluxe. When drinking gin, Bond seems to lean toward Gordon's or

## The 007 Dossier

Beefeater's. It is more than gospel that 007 likes his vodka. Smirnoff White Label tends to be his favorite, which is rated at 65.5 proof. During a party at Sir Miles Messervy's home in 1998's *The Facts Of Death*, chapter three, Bill Tanner in conversation with 007 tells him, "Go easy on the vodka, James - there're at least twenty other people here tonight who'll want some." Now this doesn't tell us that Bond has a drinking problem, only that he does enjoy his recreational popsicle from time to time.

While dining with M at Blades, M ordered a carafe of Wolfschmidt from Riga: "When M poured him three fingers from the frosted carafe Bond took a pinch of black pepper and dropped it on the surface of the vodka. The pepper slowly settled to the bottom of the glass leaving a few grains on the surface which Bond dubbed up with the tip of his finger, then he tossed the cold liquor well to the back of his throat and put the glass, with the dregs of pepper at the bottom, back on the table."

## Chapter 3: Bonded Habits

"M gave him a glance of rather ironical inquiry."

"It's a trick the Russians taught me that time you attacked me at the Embassy in Moscow," apologized Bond. "There's often quite a lot of fusel oil on the surface of this stuff - at least there used to be when it was badly distilled. Poisonous. In Russia, where you get a lot of bathtub liquor, it's an understood thing to sprinkle a little pepper in your glass. It takes the fusel oil to the bottom. I got to like the taste and now it's a habit," (*Moonraker*, chapter five). "I shouldn't have insulted the Club Wolfschmidt."

Double 0 seven does know his vodka, which is probably a very fine drink either straight or in combination. But what of that famous "Bond Martini"? We were first made aware of it in *Casino Royale*, chapter seven:

"A dry martini," he said. "One. In a deep champagne goblet."

"Oui, Monsieur."

"Just a minute. Three measures of Gordon's, one of vodka, half a measure of Kina Lillet. Shake it very well until it's ice-cold, then add a large thin slice of lemon peel. Got it?"

"Certainly Monsieur."

The barman seemed pleased with the idea. But after the martini is served to 007, he tells the barman that if he could obtain a vodka made of grain rather than potatoes the drink would be even better. But unlike Bond, most people couldn't tell the damn difference between vodka made with grain or bloody potatoes, or whether a martini had been shaken and not stirred, or care if served in a champagne goblet, tea cup or a f____ shoe box.

## *The 007 Dossier*

Later in *Casino Royale*, 007 names the martini "The Vesper" after the first Bond heroine.

In the '80s and '90s 007 still enjoys his toddy but he drinks more fine wines than he did during the '50s and '60s. When he is on assignment, Bond will order the occasional bottle of Perrier. By the turn of the century, we'll probably find 007 drinking Geritol in combination with nonfat milk or mineral water. NOT? It could happen.

Double 0 seven fundamentally stays away from the use of addictions other than alcohol. We haven't yet caught

## Chapter 3: **Bonded Habits**

him using pot or designer drugs. But he does have a habit of using Benzedrine before a tough assignment. Prior to his swim through Shark Bay in *Live And Let Die*, he takes some of these tablets. Then while at the Dreamy Pines Motor Court, 007 uses Benzedrine before taking on the likes of Horror and Sluggsy. He doesn't want to fall asleep, especially with Vivienne Michel sharing the room with him. The long swim to Dr. Shatterhand's Castle of Death requires a few tablets - in *You Only Live Twice*. While dining with M at Blades, Bond is brought an envelope, which contains powdered Benzedrine, which he mixes with his champagne and explained to M:

"Benzedrine," he said. "I rang up my secretary (Loelia Ponsonby) before dinner and asked her to wangle some out of the surgery at headquarters. It's what I shall need if I'm going to keep my wits about me tonight. It's apt to make me a bit overconfident, but that'll be a help too." He stirred the champagne with a scrap of toast so that the white powder whirled among the bubbles. Then he drank the mixture down with one long swallow. "It doesn't taste," said Bond, "and the champagne is quite excellent." (*Moonraker*, chapter five)

Even in the '90s we can find Bond using Benzedrine on assignment. SPOOKY! I doubt if 007 ever experimented with hallucinogenic drugs. I'm not going to touch that - or go there, but all is possible in the secret secret world of MI-6.

*The 007 Dossier*

## Chapter 4: Double 0 Seven = Gourmet?

Bond is quite a pick-a-dilly when it comes to his faddy likes and dislikes. He has stated that he is persnickety and old-maidish and admits to taking a near ridiculous pleasure in his eats and drinks. "It comes partly from being a bachelor, but mostly from a habit of taking a lot of trouble over details," (*Casino Royale*, chapter eight). Double 0 seven has strict likes and dislikes when it comes to food. He's a waiter's nightmare, although he wouldn't admit it. Before being seated he usually knows what he wants and asks for it in an abrupt and most authoritative fashion.

"You must forgive me," he said. "I take a ridiculous pleasure in what I eat and drink," (*Casino Royale*, chapter eight).

Although Fleming told us in chapter two of *On Her Majesty's Secret Service* that "James Bond was not a gourmet. In England he lived on grilled soles, oeufs cocotte and cold roast beef with potato salad."

Double 0 seven does enjoy breakfast and only he would insist that his special eggs be very fresh, speckled brown from French Marans hens. These special hens that lay these special eggs are owned by special friends of his special jewel of a housekeeper, May, and must be

47

## The 007 Dossier

boiled for precisely three and one-third minutes. Once May has done her duty to the egg, it is served to Bond in a dark-blue eggcup with a gold ring around the top. It greatly pleases 007 that there really is such a thing as "the perfect boiled egg." Following the super egg come two thick slices of whole wheat toast accompanied by a large pat of deep yellow Jersey butter and three squat jars which contain nothing less than "007 Super Jam" - being "Tiptree Little Scarlet's strawberry jam, Copper's Vintage Oxford marmalade and Norwegian Heather Honey from Fortnum's." Breakfast is a ritual for 007 and per chance he should miss it, his day just wouldn't go well. Besides the aforementioned, Bond must also have coffee for breakfast - but not just any coffee, it must come from De Bry on New Oxford Street and be brewed in an American Clemex, of which 007 has two large cups, strong and black and without sugar.

Bond is apparently not worried about cholesterol, even at whatever age he may be, because he loves scrambled eggs too. He usually orders scrambled eggs for lunch, rather than breakfast, because luncheon scrambled eggs are served with smoked salmon. Bond does have his own very special recipe that Fleming provides in *Thrilling Cities,* "007 in New York."

---

SCRAMBLED EGGS "JAMES BOND"
For four individualists: Bond's recipe is as follows
   12 Fresh Eggs  (We are not told if these must
         be eggs from French Marans hens.)
   Salt and Pepper
   5 to 6 Oz. Butter

---

"Break the eggs into a bowl. Beat thoroughly with a fork and season well. In a small copper (or heavy-bottomed saucepan) melt four oz. of the butter. When melted, pour in the eggs and cook over a very low heat, whisking

## Chapter 4:  *Double 0 Seven = Gourmet?*

continuously with a small egg whisk."

"While the eggs are slightly more moist than you would wish for eating, remove pan from heat, add rest of butter and continue whisking for half a minute, adding the finely chopped chives or fine herbs. Serve on hot buttered toast in individual copper dishes with pink champagne and low music."

In a recent book, Bond ate enough scrambled eggs to feed a starving platoon for a week. If we mere mortals ate so many eggs, especially from his recipe, we would find ourselves in a hospital ward, hooked up to all sorts of tubes and machines. But he is James Bond, 007, super hero.

We, the readers of the Bond adventures, are privileged to accompany 007 to the dinner table. One particular meal I found most amusing was the meal with Tiger Tanaka in *You Only Live Twice*, chapter nine. Bond "was surprised to find that the flesh was raw. He was even more surprised when...his lobster began moving off his

49

dish...and tottered off across the table. 'Good God, Tiger' Bond said, aghast. 'The damn thing's alive.'"

Our man 007 knows precisely what he wants, ALWAYS, be it while reading from a restaurant menu in France, Jamaica or America, or over the phone to room service in some hotel at any location in the world. While in Istanbul, 007 "telephoned for his breakfast" and "hoped that the exotic breakfast he ordered would not be a fiasco."

"He was not disappointed. The yogurt, in a blue china bowl, was deep yellow and with the consistency of thick cream. The green figs, ready peeled, were bursting with ripeness, and the Turkish coffee was jet black and with the burned taste that showed it had been freshly ground," (*From Russia With Love*, chapter fourteen).

Double 0 seven is not into self-discipline or self-denial. The dinner meals are always something exquisite, and he insists that his dinner dates order expensively.

"I'd made two choices," she laughed, "and either would have been delicious; but behaving like a millionaire occasionally is a wonderful treat, and if you're sure...well I'd like to start with caviar and then have a plain grilled rogon de veal with pomes souffles. And then I'd like to have fraises de bois with a lot of cream. Is it very shameless to be so certain and so expensive?' she smiled at him inquiringly.

"It's a virtue and anyway it's only a good plain wholesome meal." He turned to the maitre d'hotel. "And bring plenty of toast."

"The trouble always is," he explained to Vesper, "not how to get caviar, but how to get enough toast with it."

"Now," he turned back to the menu, "I myself will accompany Mademoiselle with the caviar, but then I would like a very small tournedos, underdone, with sauce Béarnaise and a Coeur d'artichaut. While Mademoiselle is enjoying the strawberries, I will have an avocado pear with a little French dressing. Do you approve?" (*Casino Royale*,

## Chapter 4: Double 0 Seven = Gourmet?

chapter eight).

Of course we approve, but will M when Bond turns in his expense account? M delights in a fine meal also. An entire chapter was devoted to a dinner to which M treated 007 in Moonraker. Although the descriptions were tasty, the food was entirely foreign to the avid reader. M starts the meal with caviar (no extra toast), deviled kidney with a slice of bacon, peas and new potatoes. Followed by strawberries in kirsch and a marrowbone. Bond follows suit with the same vegetables but goes for lamb cutlets, asparagus with Hollandaise sauce, a slice of pineapple and sliced smoked Scotch salmon on toast. This is not your everyday smoked salmon, for it has "the delicate glutinous texture only achieved by the Highland curers - very different from the desiccated products of Scandinavia."

It has not yet been revealed whether or not 007 eats quiche, but Bond's reputation of being a gourmet, while pretending not to be, is more than obvious. He notices and enjoys what he eats; we can't begrudge that of a man who might be tortured to death the next week, shot dead day after tomorrow, or have a coronary tonight after that date with the girl in a velvet dress with "splendid ... er... protuberances."

*Bon Apetit, Monsieur Bond.*

## The 007 Dossier

## Chapter 5: **The Bond Girls**

The Bond girls tend to have disagreeable and alarming experiences with their pre-007 male friends. Most of them have no family; they tend to be orphaned children of nature or children of criminals. Many have been employed by the Black Hat, but they tend to find this disagreeable after they have met Bond. In short, there is some mild degree of pathos in the Bond girls that differentiates them from sex objects as such.

In consequence, each one must be dealt with on a far more complex level than the ever overriding fact that she has fine, jutting, splendid, faultless, exquisite, perfectly molded, beautiful, unrestrained, perfect, firm, proud, hilly, perky, thrusting, out-thrown, unashamed, swelling, full, luscious, impertinent, delicious, hard, pointed, hillocks, deep-vallied, sexual, hard with desire, natural, apple-sized, high-riding, deeply V-ed, braless, knockout sexually, poised, discreet cleavage, well-propositioned, curved on-display breasts that are also youthful, small, slightly large, single, admirable, gentle, unmoving, splendid ... er ... protuberances, perfectly molded into a sweat-soaked T-shirt, with pink erect nipples like wild raspberries. She has become an intricate person. She must be dealt with accordingly even if she does have "emotional baggage" of a particular type. (Yeah, right.)

Of course, 007 can't be held responsible for the

*The 007 Dossier*

emotional baggage, oddities and sexual perversions that he encounters. These, most assuredly, are the author's doing. For example, the semi-rape of Vivienne Michel or the planned seduction of Tracy, his only bride to date. From the most recent book by Raymond Benson, *The Facts Of Death*, Bond says to Niki, "I'll be happy to show you what kinky means..." Yes, Bond has been known to have an enjoyable evening from time to time.

    Sex is a two-way street, though, and we can find Bond on the sidewalk at times with HIM being the sex object. Kissy Suzuki purchased a potion and pillow book to excite her intended. Tatianna was schooled in the art of seduction by SMERSH, and let's not forget Q'ute with the flat full of adult toys.

## Chapter 5: **The Bond Girls**

The Bond girls have many similar physical characteristics, blonde hair (favorite) to shades of black-brown of no-particular shade, with some black-brown headed girls even bleaching-dying their hair blonde. The hair is never, never ever coiffured and falls heavily to her shoulders or nape of her neck. Miss Moneypenny, after having brown eyes for nearly 50 years that we know of, evidently changed her eye color to blue. The power of 007 is astounding. WHAT?

The Bond girl has a wide sensual mouth and high cheekbones. She sometimes likes to sit with her legs folded under her on M's sofa. She is athletic-looking with perhaps assistance from skiing, swimming, ice skating or tennis. Most often she is five foot seven or taller and not thin but definitely not plump. Her complexion is freckle-free and most often sunburned, or at least suntanned. On many occasions, the reader is informed of "behinds" that "jutted like a man's" (*From Russia With Love*, chapter eight) or "firm and rounded as a boy's" (*Dr. No*, chapter eight).

The hands of the Bond girls are nearly always strong and practical with a firm, dry, tender, nice cool handshake. Her fingernails are usually square cut or short and unpainted. Perhaps Fleming may have overdone himself in the case of Kissy Suzuki: "her fingernails and toenails, although they were cut very short, were broken," (*You

55

## The 007 Dossier

*Only Live Twice*, chapter fourteen). Never fear though, Bond "found this rather endearing" (Ibid.).

Ian Fleming wrote detailed descriptions of the females in the adventures he authored about 007, whereas Robert Markham and John Gardner wrote fewer descriptive words of their Bond Girls. Perhaps this is good, perhaps this is modern, perhaps this is intended but it was by no means meant to be offensive with the sexual revolution and unrevolution. Raymond Benson has gotten back into the swing of Ian Fleming more or less. It is the known knowledge of men and women that women are just as interested in how a woman looks as men are. Especially in her conquest of the 20th century's foremost fantasy figure.

The Bond girls of Fleming's era wore silk shirts, pleated and straight skirts, wide belts and squared-toed shoes. These outfits were of a classic style, outside of changing fashion or fad, whereas the Bond girls of the 1990s wear jeans and denim shirts or wonderfully tailored

## Chapter 5: **The Bond Girls**

evening dresses or suits worn with elegance. And of course let's not forget the nearly always accompanying Hermes scarf worn by these trend-setting types. If 007 had kept all the Hermes scarves he had encountered over the years, he could go into competition with The Tie Rack.

The one thing that Bond Girls do have in common over the past nearly 50 years is that they tend to dress in active clothes for travel, for outdoors or for that special rendezvous, be it business, social or kinky. They are not just decorative or sexy. The Bond Girl is inside the plot rather than sitting on the sidelines as a sexy conquest. The Bond Girl has been rescued or she has rescued Bond in his time of need. She can wield a gun, throw a punch, use a cross-bow and arrow, and she has been known on more than one occasion to put karate all over a villain's body.

They are never the girl next door or the little sister, although one was the daughter of Felix Leiter. Bond girls are found wandering nude on a Caribbean beach or racing about with the sexy boom of twin exhausts bellowing from either an MG sports car or a Lancia Flaminis Zagato Spyder or encountered wearing only a black brassiere and lace panties. No matter how the inspiration is fueled, Bond is most certainly always lucky with the females. Frankly, I can't recall another character in fiction as fortunate in female conquests as Bond. He is polygamous and at the same time more than promiscuous. Nearly every personable female he encounters is ready to drop her knickers and pop into the sack with him; waitresses brush against him provocatively, other men's mistresses forget their lovers and sit beside him touching his knee, women talk to him using their "throaty voice," expensive whores offer their favors "pour amour," Chinese ladies show more leg than necessary from the split in their cheongsams, bare-breasted lap

## The 007 Dossier

dancers tease him more than is needed for any normal mortal, pretty girls bare more thigh beneath their thin skirts and advise 007 that "woman with cool palm has fire under skirt," (*No Deal, Mister Bond*, chapter twenty-three), femme fatales allow their negligees to slip off their shoulders provocatively, and last but definitely not least, bachelor chicks are fish in a barrel. The Bond girl is attracted and usually yields most willingly to his charm.

Only once that has been recorded in his assignments did 007 fail in one of his conquests. Of course, this is not counting lesbians. Although Bond has successfully managed to convert a few lesbians into heterosexuals or

## Chapter 5: *The Bond Girls*

at least into the more acceptable classification of bisexual. For example, in *Goldfinger* he converted Pussy Galore. The failed conquest mentioned above was Gala Brand, the young and exciting policewoman in *Moonraker*.

To scrutinize Bond's attitude toward women, one must reflect on the creator of the series. It was Ian Fleming who wrote and inserted his own chauvinistic ideas into 007. The first book was written and published in the 1950s, so one must keep in mind that the feminist movement of 50 years ago was far removed from the feminist movement of today. Robert Markham pretty much followed the flow of Fleming's attitudes and characterization of 007. John Gardner gave more depth and meaning to the Bond girl of the 1980s and early 1990s. Raymond Benson zeroed right in on the newest of the female roles. Maybe "heroine" would be a better descriptive word. A shared experience?

If a new reader were starting the series in chronological order, he or she would quickly realize that Bond's treatment of women could be summarized as uncaring and even ruthless. This would be undisputedly true to some degree. In deeper study though, one would have to conclude that Fleming gave his creation a job, an "aire" of not degrading women with their emotional baggage but one of protector of the weaker sex (which the modern woman could find just as chauvinistic if she wanted to). From *Casino Royale* to *The Facts Of Death* it would quickly be realized that the Bond girl could more than fend for herself. She not only is able to do such but on numerous occasions she has been known to fend for 007 as well as for country. Bond was placed in the position of St. George saving the fair damsel from the damn dragon with sometimes some very oddball situations and solutions. But this is why he is James Bond, 007.

One could see Bond as a romantic, even though he keeps the involvement to a short-term fantasy as such, but this is perhaps the reason he is a fantasy. The reader must

59

*The 007 Dossier*

remember that the Bond girls do not seem to mind this, as each one is independent and depicted as not looking for an everlasting swan song. Apparently it would seem that 007 isn't looking for anything permanent either.

## Chapter 6: Is This The One?

We are aware of more than one occasion when this thought passed through Bond's mind. And we're sure the thought has passed through more than one his exciting female companions' minds.

So what of matrimony for Bond?

While chatting in Nassau with his friend the governor, Bond said that if he were to marry, she would have to be an airline hostess. When asked why, he answered, "It would be fine to have a pretty girl always tucking you up and bringing you drinks and hot meals and asking if you had everything you wanted. And they're always smiling and wanting to please. If I don't find an airline hostess, there'll be nothing for it but marry a Japanese. They seem to have the right ideas too." (*Quantum Of Solace, For Your Eyes Only*).

007 may fantasize about airline hostesses and Japanese women, but a relationship with Betty Crocker wouldn't last more

## The 007 Dossier

than a fortnight.

Bond does think a lot about marriage. In *Casino Royale* he was in deep thought about asking Vesper Lynd to marry him, but as the novel progresses she turns out to be a double agent - and she commits suicide. This must have hurt 007 deeply because in *On Her Majesty's Secret Service* we are informed that Bond paid an annual visit to her gravesite. Then there was Tiffany Case from *Diamonds Are Forever* with whom he shared his flat off King's Road - until clashes between Tiffany and May, 007's housekeeper, upset Bond's very organized life.

The next woman was Tracy from *On Her Majesty's Secret Service* whom he actually did marry. However, she was murdered by Blofeld shortly after the ceremony. Then in the following book, Bond lived with a Japanese woman named Kissy Suzuki for a year. Was this a guilt trip, remorse or just the natural flow of hormones? Maybe this affair didn't count because we are told that Bond had amnesia and couldn't remember. He eventually leaves her to go to Mother Russia, not knowing that Kissy is pregnant with his child.

And what of James Jr. or little Kissy? Did he/she fend for him/herself? Was he/she put up for adoption? Did he/she follow in Bond's footsteps and become a secret service agent? Supposedly, 007 was never aware of the child. No father figure? Not cool. The child would be in his mid-thirties now. I'm curious.

Bond said of the affair in general, "...shunned the mise-in-scene for each of three acts in the play - the meeting at the party, the restaurant, the taxi, his flat, then the weekend by the sea, then the flat again, then the furtive alibis and the final angry farewell on some doorstep in the rain," (*Casino Royale*, chapter twenty-two).

And again, after Bond dropped off Jill Masterton at the railroad station, after what surely must be defined as a lustful affair, we are informed that

"... the girl was starved for physical love. She had woken

## Chapter 6: Is This The One?

him twice more in the night with soft demanding caresses, saying nothing, just reaching for his hard lean body..." "Bond had taken her to the station and had kissed her once hard on the lips and had gone away. It hadn't been love, but a quotation had come into Bond's mind as his cab moved out of Pennsylvania Station. "Some love is fine, some love is rust. But the finest, cleanest love is lust." Neither had had regrets. Had they committed sin? If so, which one? A sin against chastity? Bond smiled to himself. There was a quotation for that too, and from a saint - Saint Augustine: "Oh Lord, give me chastity. But don't give it yet," (*Goldfinger*, chapter five).

In book after book, 007 has thoughts about the bliss that marriage could give him. For example, about a vine-covered cottage in the country. It was not to be. In *The Facts Of Death*, chapter three, we find Bond sitting in his Bentley, cursing himself for having such thoughts and wishing the rain would wash away the melancholy that he has had to ultimately accept. And as recently as 1993 and 1994, 007 shared his flat in London with Flicka.

But the fact is, no female on earth is going to accept 007's way of bringing home the bacon

*The 007 Dossier*

## Chapter 7: **Office Hanky Panky**

When 007 is not saving Queen/King and country, he has office hours from 10 a.m. to 6 p.m., five days a week on the fourth floor of the SIS Building.

In *Zero Minus Ten*, chapter three, we learn that, "Bond has never been keen on office decoration. The one piece of artwork on display was an obscure artist's watercolor of the clubhouse at the Royal St. George Golf Course. The one framed photograph on the desk featured Bond and his closest American friend, former CIA agent, Felix Leiter, sitting in a bar in New York City. It was an old photo, and the two men looked surprised and slightly drunk. It never failed to make Bond smile."

Bond does have a desk in a more than mysterious building near Regents Park. The "Front" for this, the most top secret depository has had its name changed more than a few times over the past few years. A hard-nosed bloke using only the name "M" for many years headed this "Front." It was later to be headed by a "soft-nosed" bloke using the name "M," which we will go into later. But, we should imagine that this cover is justifiably blown, because every undercover agency on the bloody planet must know that it's really the headquarters for MI-6, the British Secret Service.

Be what it may. It's James Bond's home base, where, when not on assignment he puts in a dull day reading and

## *The 007 Dossier*

expediting interoffice memos, relieved only by practice with firearms, new gadgets from Q Branch, training in unarmed skills of close-hand combat and the silent kill.

But then, there is the occasional pleasant office flirtation, of which Bond is not apprehensive to dip his pen into the company ink every now and again. As a pastime, it's still better than shooting rabbits.

At the office, Miss Moneypenny, M's private secretary, would throughout the years be an easy conquest for 007. When we first make her acquaintance in *Casino Royale* "she would have been desirable but only for eyes which were cool and direct and quizzical," (*Casino Royale*, chapter three). The following year in *Live And Let Die*,

## Chapter 7: Office Hanky Panky

chapter two, she is the "desirable Miss Moneypenny" with "an encouraging smile." Several years later in *Diamonds Are Forever*, chapter three, Bond smiles into her "warm brown eyes." In *From Russia With Love*, chapter twelve, her eyes had that "look of excitement and secret knowledge as she smiled" at 007. In 1961 *Thunderball*, chapter one, we find her warming considerably as she "often dreamed hopelessly about Bond." And then in *License Renewed*, chapter two, we are told that "There had been a special bantering relationship between them for years, yet Bond had never fully realized how much the able and neat Moneypenny doted on him."

With the release of *For Special Services* in 1982, which surely would put Miss Moneypenny at a pretend age of between 55 and 60, she is in a state of jealousy over a certain "cute little girl from Q-Branch," chapter four. Then a full nine years later in *The Man From Barbarosa*, chapter two, Miss Moneypenny would be 64 to 69 years of pretend age as "Bond leans across the desk to kiss her lightly on the forehead."

"You're like a sister to me, Penny," Bond smiled.

"I don't feel sisterly." Moneypenny never bothered to hide the deep passion she nursed for Bond.

Bond answered, "Oh come on Penny, I don't want to add incest to injury."

In conversation with Miss Moneypenny in *The Facts Of Death* published in 1998 and written by Raymond Benson, Bond tells her, "I don't have a type," which will be shown in the CHICK CHART.

Miss Moneypenny, in her nearly 50 years of service with MI-6, has gotten in some good lines. In *Tomorrow Never Dies* when the new female M is telling 007 to pump an old girlfriend for some needed information, Moneypenny whispers to Bond, "I suppose you'll have to decide how much pumping is needed." Bond whispers back, "If only that were true of me and you." (chapter four).

## The 007 Dossier

Of course Miss Moneypenny's demeanor most of the time is entirely no-nonsense, but when 007 was in attendance her blue eyes betrayed her inner feelings. "Throughout their years of working together, the relationship had been mutually flirtatious," with an occasional off the cuff zinger, but it had grown to one of a "comfortable friendship."

Something has happened here - did you pick it up? Miss Moneypenny's warm brown eyes have now turned blue. Perhaps she had been fitted with a pair of contacts that changed the color of her eyes. Maybe she's been reading Bond and discovered that he has a preference for blue eyes. Who knows. (Could a tummy-tuck be far away?)

Miss Moneypenny was one of the few women at MI-6 who didn't mind being called MISS. Yes, there were no Ms for this MISS.

When John Gardner wrote *Nobody Lives Forever* this MISS was no longer just office decoration. It's too bad that Miss Moneypenny missed having grandchildren because she now had a story to tell.

After Sir Miles Messervy left MI-6 for retirement, Moneypenny found that she got along rather well with the new M, and that her job was still a pleasure. She decided not to transfer out. "It was a good thing, for many believed that SIS wouldn't function properly without Miss Moneypenny's vast knowledge of the entire organization and its history." (*Zero Minus Ten*, chapter three).

Besides Miss Moneypenny, Bond has had a string of personal secretaries. Loelia Ponsonby is the first we know about. Truly she can't be counted as another doll in Bond's "playpen" though. Ponsonby was described as "tall and dark with reserved, unbroken beauty" with a "touch of sternness." We are informed of "determined assaults on her virtue" by Bond and his double O counterparts. She had abandoned MI-6 and "had at last left to marry a dull, but worthy rich member of the Baltic

## Chapter 7: Office Hanky Panky

Exchange." (*Moonraker*, chapter one). Right on Loelia!
    She was replaced by a secretary who looked like a permanent tease to the Double O Boys. Mary Goodnight, an ex-Wren with blue-black hair, blue eyes and (get this) 37-22-35 measurements, was a honey. There was a private five-pound sweep in the section as to who would "sack her first," (*On Her Majesty's Secret Service*, chapter six). Bond was the co-favorite for a time, but after 007's marriage to

Tracy he dropped out of the running for a while. Don't concern yourself too much with this, because in *The Man With The Golden Gun* Mary Goodnight, after dying her hair a golden blond, ended up being the Bond Girl. We never did find out if 007 picked up the five-pound sweep.
    From *Zero Minus Ten*, chapter three, we learn much more about Bond's perks at work.
"His personal assistant (Bond couldn't help still thinking of

## The 007 Dossier

her as a "secretary"), Ms. (not Miss) Helena Marksbury, was busy holding down the fort. Helena worked for all of the Double Os, having been with SIS for about a year. Since the days of Loelia Ponsonby and Mary Goodnight, there had been a steady succession of lissome blondes, brunettes and redheads occupying the front desk. As for Helena Marksbury, she was a brunette with large green eyes. She was bright, quick-witted and damnably attractive. Bond thought that had she not been his personal assistant, the lovely Helena would have made an enjoyable dinner date...with an option for breakfast the next morning."

In the newest book *The Facts Of Death*, chapter three, we find Bond and Helena at the old M's house on a patio. After an intimate kiss, she pulls away breathlessly and says, "I know this isn't sexual harassment, but I'd better point out that you're my boss, James." Back in his Bentley, "He cursed himself for what had just happened. He knew better than to get involved with women at the office. If only she wasn't so bloody attractive!

What was it in him that made him want to seduce every woman he found desirable? Temporary recreational love was satisfying and always had been, but it certainly didn't fill a greater need Bond had. Was it possible that what he craved was a woman to love - really love - in order to fill that hole? The scars on his heart were many and deep."

Back at the office and out of the secretary pool a

## Chapter 7: Office Hanky Panky

few years back we are introduced to what is most assuredly inner-departmental hanky panky.

The aforementioned "cute little girl from Q Branch" was one Ann Reilly, otherwise known as Q'ute. Bond has a relationship with her in *License Renewed* and in *For Special Services* they are "occasional lovers." Then finally in *Role Of Honor*, "Bond caught her eye and smiled, but she merely looked through him, coldly, as though he did not exist" (chapter three).

## The 007 Dossier

We know little about her, other than that she had straw-colored hair, wore velvet and had a flat full of "adult toys." We are not fully enlightened as to the use of these adult toys. We, the readers, are finally going to learn more about 007 and perhaps his knowledge and skill in the operation of these toys. HIs skill at kinky hanky panky, but DAMN!! It wasn't within our power to continue the paragraph.

On many occasions, we are informed that M strongly disapproved of Bond's womanizing, but apparently this didn't keep 007 from enjoying a little hanky panky at the office, as we well know. (Will wonders never cease.)

## Chapter 8: **M & M's**

Most assuredly, James Bond has met the weirdest of the weird. But why does he do it, this Secret Service business? Out of friendship for M? This doesn't seem very likely. If anything, M is Bond's foremost adversary. More than once, a certain love-hate relationship has flared between them.

M is the head of the British Secret Service, otherwise known as MI-6. He commands the organization from behind a desk at a large building near Regent's Park. As a cover story, he appears to the world to be the head of a firm called "Universal Export." The cover name was changed in *The Man With The Golden Gun* to "Transworld Consortium." And then again in *License Renewed* to "Transworld Export Ltd." To his staff, he is the "Perennial Skipper" or the "Old Man." M was

73

## The 007 Dossier

always a very secretive person; it was many years before we learned his full name. I would not be betraying any confidences if I were to reveal his name, for it can be found between the pages of the 007 books if one cared to look for it.

"Admiral Sir Miles Messervy" is rather heroic in the way of the Old School. He has "frosty, damnable clear grey eyes," smokes a pipe and has the use of an ancient Rolls Royce. He is a retired Vice-Admiral and relishes "...the certain prospect of becoming Fifth Sea Lord in order to take over the Secret Service." He lives in London and also keeps residence at a small Regency house on the Crown Lands near Windsor Forest. M had named this place "Quarterdeck," but he would prefer to live by the sea. At Quarterdeck, guests announce their arrival by ringing a brass bell.

Once inside, against a background of naval prints and M's own watercolors of English wild orchids, guests may be offered a small glass of Marsala, a very nasty Algerian wine, and a cheap black cheroot.

It is not surprising that M disapproved of 007's womanizing, for he was born during the Victorian Era. M also disapproved of Bond's choice of drink and his 60 to 70 cigarette-a-day smoking habit. But, all in all, M is a fairly decent sort of bloke for Bond to work for, because he did show 007 special consideration, more than he did perhaps the other 00 boys. (Especially considering the fact that Bond tried to kill M in *The Man With The Golden Gun*; but actually Bond redeemed himself in *Colonel Sun* by saving M.) In *License Renewed*, this is clarified by the following when M tells Bond, "Changing

## Chapter 8: M & M's

world, changing times, James," when breaking the news that the elite Double 0 status-which meant being licensed to kill in the line of duty-was being abolished. "Fools of politicians have no idea of our requirements. As far as I'm concerned, 007, you will remain 007. I shall take full responsibility for you, and you will, as ever, accept orders and assignments only from me. There are moments when this country needs a troubleshooter-a blunt instrument-and by heaven, it's going to have one. They can issue their pieces of bumf and abolish the Double 0 section. We can simply change its name. It will now be the Special Section, and you are it. Understand, 007?" (*License Renewed*, chapter two).

Even so, devotion to King/Queen and country can't possibly be the reason M took on this most exacting and demanding job as Head of the British Secret Service. Bond and M have clashed on numerous occasions, and I believe that to a certain degree M mistrusts 007. To be fair to M, I suppose that he is the closest thing to a sort of Dr. Watson or Tonto that the Bond novels have to offer, as M is the only other character who has put in an appearance in all the 007 adventures.

M is an unmarried widower. He has two daughters; the oldest named Haley was once married to an American. She has two children and their names are Charles and Lynne. In *The Facts Of Death*, chapter three, Haley comes on a little strong for Bond's liking, and he tells Tanner, "She is a divorcee with two children and that's enough to keep me away." I think most of us know from reading *You Only Live Twice* that 007 doesn't want anything to do with kids. Not once in any of the stories has Bond been at the dinner table with friends and family - and played "pass the baby."

Something must keep M from going bonkers. Like Bond, he is ex-Navy - and we all know all about ex-Naval men. However, age may play a part in this. M is most highly moral and scrupulous in matters of sex and as of yet, it has

## *The 007 Dossier*

not been disclosed that M patronizes single bars or calls 1-900 numbers.

When Bond returns from assignment in *Cold Fall*, he is informed that M has retired and the new M requests his presence NOW. This is after Bond has worked with Sir Miles Messervy for at least 43 years that we know about,

and he is told "...the new M's a woman." Whereby 007 says, "Then she can't be as bad as the old M." (*Cold Fall*, chapter two).

We, the followers of Bond, have accompanied him on 27 full-length adventures and eight short stories with the old M as head of MI-6. (Myself, I prefer the title MI-6 for the British Secret Service rather than the SIS or anything else they want to call it.) Changing times! But we actually knew very little about him. In the five books with the new M at the helm, already we have learned quite a bit about her, and I myself like this.

Nicknamed "Lady Precious Stream" by the wags for

## Chapter 8: **M & M's**

her ability to curse like a deckhand "and Bond answered back, 'heard it all before, seen it, done it.'" (*Cold Fall*, chapter two).

In *Goldeneye*, chapter seven, Bill Tanner, who had reluctantly stayed on after almost resigning after his job title had been changed from "Chief of Staff" to "Senior Analyst," referred to the new M as "The Evil Queen of Numbers." She torted back, "I happen to believe in numbers. Numbers are more accurate than human beings." Later in conversation with 007 she says, "You don't really like me, do you Bond? You see me as a jumped-up pocket calculator." And Bond simply nodded his answer.

The new M believed Bond to be a "cold-hearted bastard" and a "sexist misogynist dinosaur" along with being a "relic from the Cold War." (*Goldeneye*, chapter eight).

In *Goldeneye*, chapter seven, the new M got off one of the best lines in the book. "Unlike the American Government, we prefer not to get bad news from CNN."

Small in stature, and of course smart and alert, she had the habit of drumming her fingers on the desk. She

77

could take nothing at face value. This could be from her background as an analyst. She has the ability to hmpf, huff and grunt like the old M. Perhaps this is a requirement for the job. Unlike the old M, she smokes cigarettes rather than a pipe. I haven't found out yet if these are custom-made, hand-made or specially made for her. The new M has the habit of raising an eyebrow as Sir Miles did. She prefers bourbon to cognac.

Although the female M's eyes hinted at perhaps some distant Asian blood, she has blue eyes that are very striking, cool with streaks of white in the irises. Her hair is cut short, grayish, and she has a "rather severe face." The new M's age is stated at the high side of 50. Her charisma commanded attention. She is neither tall nor slender. Her name is Barbara Mawdsley.

She stated that if Bond thought that she didn't "have the balls to send a man out to die on some dodgy foreign field, then your instincts are dead wrong." She isn't gullible or squeamish and has no trouble assigning "dirty works" to the Double Os. Bond lets her know, "Ma'am, I've never forgotten that a license to kill is also a certificate to die." (*Goldeneye*, chapter eight).

The old M, Sir Miles, enlightens 007 that the New Lady M's bark is worse than her bite, (*Cold Fall*, chapter 26). We are informed in *Tomorrow Never Dies*, chapter four, that she is extremely tough and had already gotten Bond's admiration in mere months of working with her. From *Facts Of Death*, chapter three, after a social gathering at the old M's home, her lover is murdered. Bond is astonished that she could be romantically involved and have a sex life. Could she be the mother figure Bond never had? I doubt it but it is something to ponder. (It could happen!)

All civil servants have to change the decorations of their new offices at the taxpayers expense when they get a promotion, and Barbara Mawdsley is no different. Since taking over the old M's position as head of SIS or MI-6

## Chapter 8: **M & M's**

(whatever), she has changed Sir Miles' office drastically. No longer the "Captain's Quarters" of a navy vessel, the new look was "more akin to a posh psychiatrist's office. Sparse, ultramodern furnishings filled the place with a stark black-and-white scheme that was surprisingly pleasing to the eye." (*Zero Minus Ten*, chapter three).

Lots of glass, shiny metal with black leather, accented with artwork of all types - and behind the desk, an original Kandinsky adorned the wall. *Goldeneye*, chapter three, tells us the new office had a "Scandinavian influence, posture improving chairs." The now new black desk was clutter free and had several color-coded phones and a large computer with a monitor.

I like the new M, but a black desk, glass, chrome, black leather and a Kandinsky? BORING.

We, the readers of 007, never expected change. Most of us look forward to the new novels from year to year. We didn't expect CHANGE. It was supposedly always going to be James Bond, M, Moneypenny, Tanner, Q, May, Leiter and even Q'ute, besides the femme fatale and whatever evil no-good-nic who came along. But change? Okay, but keep James Bond, 007.

The followers of Bond seem to treat the adventures as lighthearted fun

## The 007 Dossier

jokes; we tend to enjoy his likes and dislikes as much as our own. We hiss and boo his adversaries, look forward and whistle when the femme fatale makes her debut, groan and moan when he is captured, wince when he is tortured, find admiration when he escapes and cheer at his successes.

Bond is battling to preserve the life of the Free World against an assortment of evildoers and no-good-nics who wish to destroy freedom of choice and put the world into a state of terminal confusion. In each adventure, the villain is only interested in achieving power, while 007 is merely, up to the moment of accepting the assignment, interested in enjoying this life to its fullest.

## Chapter 9: The Bond Mobiles

Bond's lust and passion do not zero in and thrive on iced vodka and femme fatales alone. He loves cars - fast cars, cars with toys and gadgets, cars that are customized and personalized for his most demanding needs and requirements. The first of these Bond Mobiles is described in *Casino Royale*, chapter five. It was "...one of the last of the 4-1/2 liter Bentleys with the supercharger by Anherst Villiers."

We are told that he purchased the car in 1933, but we could logically prove that it was purchased the year of his birth. Now, however you look at it, that's thinking just a little too far ahead. If we use the date of 1924 as the year of his birth, we find that at the age of nine, he purchased the Bentley - although it may take a little longer to learn to drive at that age, and then perhaps get specially made blocks to put on his shoes so that he could reach the pedals. Be that as it may! We do know in both *From A View To A Kill* and *Role Of Honor* that he was able to drive it to Paris for a most "memorable evening" and then to Lake Geneva for that rendezvous with the waitress from Lakeside Cafe. I myself can believe that a 17-year-old boy would fib about being 18 or 19 in order to be accepted into the Navy, but a nine-year-old lad just isn't going to get a driver's license in any country that I know of. Say what?

In regards to his Bentley, Bond "...had kept it in

## *The 007 Dossier*

careful storage through the war. It was still serviced every year, and in London, a former Bentley mechanic who worked in a garage near Bond's flat tended it with jealous care. Bond drove it hard and well and with a sensual pleasure. It was a battleship - grey convertible coupe which really did convert, and it was capable of touring at 90 with 30 an hour in reserve." (*Casino Royale*, chapter five).

    Double 0 seven kept this Bentley for at least 22 years after he had purchased it. We know of at least two severe crashes with the Bentley - in both *Casino Royale* when Le Chiffre caused an accident with that carpet of spikes, and again in *Moonraker* when Hugo Drax arranged for those heavy rolls of newsprint to be released on him. At the closing of *Moonraker*, Bond is in the process of purchasing a 1953 Mark VI Bentley with an open touring body. It is of course battle-ship grey, as was the old one. "She is sold. On one condition. That you get her over to the Ferry Terminal at Calais by tomorrow evening." (chapter twenty-five). 007's

## Chapter 9:  The Bond Mobiles

plans never did mature as he wished, and I wonder if that salesman is still waiting for him?

Several years later in *Goldfinger*, 007 drives his choice of either a Jaguar 3.4 or an Aston-Martin DBIII, furnished by the motorpool of Q Branch of the Secret Service. He chose the DBIII because of numerous extras that Q Branch had built into the car. For the next few years, nothing is mentioned about cars other than the occasional taxi or lifts.

Then in *Thunderball*, Bond owned "...the most selfish car in England. It was a Mark II Continental Bentley that some rich idiot had married to a telephone pole on the Great West Road. Bond had bought the bits for L1500, and Rolls had straightened the bend in the chassis and fitted new clockwork - the Mark IV engine with 9.5 compression. Then Bond had gone to Mulliners with L3000, which was half his total capital, and they had sawed off the old cramped sports saloon body and had fitted a trim, rather square convertible

## The 007 Dossier

two-seater affair, power-operated, with only two large armed bucket seats in black leather. The rest of the blunt end was all knife-edged, rather ugly, trunk. The car was painted in rough, not gloss, battleship gray (could this be different than battleship-grey) and the upholstery was black morocco. She went like a bird and a bomb and Bond loved her more than all the women in his life at present rolled, if that was feasible, together." (chapter seven).

In 1968, Bond still owned the Continental Bentley, which he was driving the most benign day when he uncovered the kidnapping of M by that rascal Colonel Sun. Then in 1981, 20 years after purchase, "With fuel costs running high and the inevitability that they would continue to do so, Bond had allowed the beloved old Mark II Continental Bentley to go the way of its predecessor, the 4.5 liter Bentley." (*License Renewed*, chapter two).

We the readers are not informed if it also went to its grave at Maidstone or not.

"Some eyebrows were raised at his choice of a foreign car, when all the pressure was on to buy British, but Bond shrugged it off by pointing to the fact that it was a British specialist firm which carried out the particularly complex and sophisticated personalization — such as the digital instrument display, the cruise control system and several other pieces of magic made possible by British know-how and the mighty microchip."

"He did not mention the month during which the car had been taken over by the Multinational Communication Control System (CCS) Company, who added some of their own standard refinements - security devices which would make Q Branch's mouths water. Bond reasoned that it was his car, and he, not Q Branch - which was under severe financial restraint anyway - would decide what features should be incorporated. On several occasions he had seen Major Boothroyd, the Armorer, nosing around the Saab; and it was now commonplace for him to catch members of

## Chapter 9: The Bond Mobiles

Q Branch - the "gee-whiz" technicians of the Service - taking a close look. None of them ever mentioned the things they could not fail to notice, such as the bulletproof glass, the steel-reinforced ram bumpers and the heavy-duty tires, self-sealing even after being hit by bullets. There were other niceties though which nobody in Q Branch could detect without bringing out specialist gear."

"The Saab now suited Bond's purposes and was easily converted from gasoline to gasohol if the fuel situation became even more critical; the consumption was low in relation to speed; while the turbo gave that extra needed thrust always needed in a tricky situation." (*License Renewed*, chapter two).

Double 0 seven nicknamed the Saab "The Silver Beast," but for Bond to buzz about in a Saab, even with all those wonderful gadgets and toys, is just a little unbelievable for the avid 007 fan. He kept his two previous cars for an average of 21 years each. The diehard readers of the Bond books were undoubtedly surprised to find that he traded the car after having it for only three years. (Perhaps some of his reasoning was that he suspected, the same as some of his readers, that he was soon to pass on a real SAAB-STORY.)

In 1984, *Role Of Honor*, chapter two Bond came into a "...legacy. It arrived, literally out of the blue, in a thick manila envelope with a Sydney postmark, and fell with a heavy plop through his letter box early in the following November. The letter was from a firm of solicitors who for many years acted for the younger brother of Bond's father, an uncle whom Bond had never seen. Uncle Bruce, it appeared, had died a wealthy man, leaving every penny of his estate to his nephew James, who hitherto had enjoyed a little private money. Now his fortunes were drastically changed."

"The whole settlement came to around a quarter of a million sterling. There was one condition to the will. Old

85

## The 007 Dossier

Uncle Bruce had a sense of humor and decreed that his nephew should spend at least one hundred thousand pounds within the first four months in 'a frivolous and extravagant manner.'"

"Bond did not have to think twice about how he might best comply with such an eccentric proviso. Bentley motor cars had always been a passion, and he had sorely resented getting rid of the old models that he had owned, driven, enjoyed and loved. During the last year he had genuinely lusted after the brand-new Bentley Mulsanne Turbo. When the will was finally through probate, he took himself straight down to Jack Barclay's showrooms in Berkeley square and ordered the hand-built car — in his old favorite British Racing Green, with a magnolia interior." (What? Not Battleship Gray-Grey?)

"One month later, he visited the Rolls-Royce Car Division at Crewe, spending a pleasant day with the chief executive and explaining that he wanted no special technology built into the car apart from a small concealed weapon compartment and a long-range telephone, which would be provided by the security experts at CCS. The Mulsanne Turbo was delivered in the late spring and Bond - having put down the full price with the order - was happy to get rid of the remaining statutory thirty thousand pounds plus by spending it on friends, mainly female, and himself, in a spree of high living such as he had not enjoyed for many years."

Here's hoping 007 can find a former or even a present Bentley mechanic who will take care of this Bentley with the "jealous care" with which the former mechanic tended the old ones. Judging from the treatment the new Bentley Turbo received in *Role Of Honor*, it looks like it'll be a tough job getting 21 years out of this bloody car.

Then in *Goldeneye* in 1995, we find 007 scooting around the south of France in an Aston-Martin DB-5. The vintage of a DB-5 is 1963 to '65 and they had a much more

## Chapter 9: The Bond Mobiles

powerful engine than the older DB-3, which he was issued in *Goldfinger* in 1959. The DB-3 is an out and out sports racing machine, like a Cobra, built between 1952 and 1955. The DB-3 would have been street illegal in most countries. (In the movies showing the *Goldfinger* car, they used a DB-5 for filming.)

The DB-3, DB-4, DB4GT and DB-5 are as different cars as a Jaguar XJS compared to a Jaguar XK8. The book *Goldfinger* was written in 1959, and there wasn't a DB5. The DB-4 was built from 1958 to 1963, and the DB-4 GT from 1959 to 1963, which was replaced by the DB-5 from 1963 to 1965. So my conclusion is that Q Branch had a fleet of Aston-Martins for the Double O Boys to tool around in. Got it? Well I'm glad that's finally cleared up.

In *Tomorrow Never Dies*, chapter four (1997), besides purchasing the holiday retreat in Jamaica in *Zero Minus Ten*, chapter one (1997), we also learn that "When Q Branch decided to work with BMW and other automobile manufacturers, some of the company Aston-Martins were sold to the highest bidders. Bond had outbid Bill Tanner for the car (DB-5) by five thousand pounds. His (Bond's) personal mechanic, Melvin Heckman, kept it in superb shape and also allowed Bond to store it in a private garage."

(Apparently Bond has his flat in London, a holiday getaway in Jamaica, the Bentley and the always-exciting Aston-Martin. What's he keeping at Shamelady? Perhaps a Range Rover? Could it be? James Bond, 007 = Yuppie?? Oh, please NOT - No Gucci slip-on alligator, Ralph Lauren polo shirts or Louis Vuitton Luggage. Okay?)

James Bond isn't afraid to let the Aston-Martin show its stuff, because in *Tomorrow Never Dies*, chapter four, Bond drove the car to Oxford and surprised his language professor by arriving an hour early in the classic. In *Goldeneye*, chapter three, Bond "swung the old Aston-Martin DB-5 into a hairpin bend on the Grand Corniche, the highest of those roads which run parallel to the coast,

## The 007 Dossier

in the foothills of the Alps Maritimes."

"He had almost forgotten what a joy it was to drive the Aston-Martin, which handled like the thoroughbred it was." In minutes, he was snaking the curves in an out and out competition with a yellow Ferrari 355. Go Bond. Double 0 seven informs his passenger, " 'Speed, my dear Caroline, is one of the few aphrodisiacs left to mankind.' He gave her a wicked smile, the cruel mouth lifting in pleasure while his startling ice-blue eyes twinkled."

In 1998, Bond is still driving a Bentley for his personal use, but is given a company car which is actually the most outrageous, fantastic car of his career, the Jaguar XK-8 Coupe. The car has so many modifications that the readers tend to skip over some of them the first time they read of them in chapter two of *The Facts Of Death*.

From the moment Double 0 seven heard that Q Branch had gotten the car for company use, he took an unprecedented interest in what features would be incorporated into this high-eye, high-priced, high-speed, high-tech machine.

"I'm sorry to say that M has decided that you are to be the lucky man to test-drive it in the field," Boothroyd told 007.

Whereby Bond asked, "When can I have it?"

Major Boothroyd had equipped the XK-8 with some very super special toys. He had "...coated the car with chobam armor, which is impenetrable," and also has the ability to "...deflect the bullets." Q told Bond "...the metal is self-healing." The body of the sleek car we are informed "...can heal itself." And to top that off, there is a solid blue base finish with a zinc coating giving it a glamorous sheen.

Of course the engine and transmission had been entirely reworked to give Bond that extra whoop when needed. Propelling the special XK-8 over 155 mph with some in reserve, using a full 400 BHP. (This should do until Bond is able to transport himself via fiber optics.)

## Chapter 9: The Bond Mobiles

Among the other custom-made, specially made or hand-made toys on this distinctive, unique Jag were the following (and this is just mentioning a few; the list could go on for several pages): interchangeable license plates, the ability to change serial numbers, a GPS navigation system allowing the car to drive itself, heat seeking rockets and cruise missiles, a flying scout that can send targets back to the driver with the ability to drop mines, a deployable air bag allowing the driver to literally smother someone, special trick Hologram lights and, get this, an electronically sensitive pigment which allows the XK-8 to change colors (green, blue, red, whatever). It could happen.

The car is really only a two-place car, so if Bond wants to play anaconda on a date, she's out of luck or in luck, not much escape room in this pleasure-mobile. Behind the wheel of this new high-priced, high eye, high-speed, high-tech XK-8 - 007's success at eluding sticky situations may not surpass the combined abilities of Barney Oldfield, Carroll Shelby, Grahm Hill, Mario Andretti, Niki Lauda and Batman, but Bond is good, very good.

## *The 007 Dossier*

Now at last there is a Bond-Mobile that will allow 007 to kick some asphalt, well into the new millennium and beyond.

## Chapter 10: *Rogues, Scamps & No-Good-Nics*

Undoubtedly, Bond enjoys his cars, custom-made cigarettes, and his booze, clothes and female companionship. Although these are not the substance of the 007 novels. The no-good-nic is the "why" of 007; otherwise Bond would only be a playboy. What is the WHY of the villain? POWER. Power distinguishes him. As Dr. No said, "That is why I am here. That is why you are here. That is why here exists." (*Dr. No*, chapter fifteen).

The primary differences between Bond and the villain is that the Badies are willing to allow the death of many people and mass destruction to achieve their ends. Whereas 007 is concerned with the saving of property and the death of the villain. (No villain has ever served time in the slammer, other than Rosa Klebb, and she was only an employee of SMERSH,, and Koyla Chernov who was taken into custody.) Once 007 and the villain have locked horns, the only form of power that exists is the power to survive; the power of life and death.

Most definitely there is a preliminary to the Bond adventures. The villain has done many an evil deed and has many a nasty thing planned for the future. Of course, these normally build up to the fight to the death of 007 and evildoer. The simple difference between Bond and the villain is that 007 is the clean-cut all-British lad and the villain is a deformed monster. In reading Bond books, one quickly

## The 007 Dossier

learns that no Englishman does anything naughty. The basic villain can always be American, Bulgarian, Chingro, Chinese, Corsican, Cuban, German, Irish, Italian, Japanese, Korean, Russian, Sicilian, Spanish-American, Turkish or Yugoslavian, but he is never, neverever English.

Goldfinger is thought to be British, but actually he holds a Nassavian passport and is found to be a displaced Balt. Red Grant speaks as an English gentleman so that he can pass himself off as a British Secret Service Agent, but he comes from Ireland and has a German father. Sir Hugo Drax at first appears to be a different matter, a national British hero, member of Blades, but he turns out to be a German by the name of Hugo von der Drache. In *License Renewed* it is revealed that the Laird of Murcaldy is suspect,

## Chapter 10: *Rogues, Scamps & No-Good-Nics*

and later he is disclosed and exposed as son of the black sheep of the family and had a Sicilian mother. But never believe they won't keep trying. Guy Thackery in the 1997 accounting in *Zero Minus Ten* is British by ancestry. His family since 1850 had commanded a shipping firm in Hong Kong known as Eurasia Enterprises Ltd. When Bond first met him, we were put off the track by the man's firm, dry grip - usually not allowed for a scamp in the assignments of 007, James Bond, half-Swiss, half-Scot.

Yes, James Bond has encountered them all, gangsters of the extraordinaire, master spies, thugs, archcriminals, scamps, rogues, badies, no-good-nics, not to mention by name a large number of just plain kooks! If the collection of adversaries were not enough to contend with, Bond has also had to joust with numerous very powerful and devious organizations. In no particular order, these have been: SMERSH, a secret section of the Soviet government, fully known as Smiert Spionam, which roughly translates "Death to Spies;" SPECTRE, which is the mischievous contraction for "The Special Executive for Counterintelligence, Terrorism, Revenge and Extortion;" Chinese Triads; C.O.L.D., "Children of the Last Days;" the U.S.S.R. on several occasions; the Spangled Mob; Scaramanga; Red China, the National Socialist Action Army, whose wish it was to bring back the "Fourth Reich;" the Monad, Castro and numerous self-employed nuts.

Bond's usual adversary is either monstrous or uncouth in more than one aspect. The reader finds them either believable or totally unbelievable. There are no zones of gray-grey in Bond's adversaries. Whether placed in alphabetical or chronological order, problems arise in discussing them. Each seems more villainous and devious than the previous.

In a sampling of 007's adversaries, each reader of the Bond books seems to have his or her favorite. Among my favorites are Mr. Big, Hugo Drax, Goldfinger, Blofeld,

93

## The 007 Dossier

Colonel Sun, Dr. No, the Ice King, Alec Trevelyan = 006 (Janus), the Spangled Mob, Guy Thackery, Scaramanga, Anton Murik, Le Chiffre, Oddjob, Rosa Klebb - Red Grant, Kolya Chernov, Elliot Carver, Tamil Rahani. Oh, hell, I just enjoyed them all.

Among those listed may not be your favorite, but I found each only more interesting than the last. Rather than discuss them all, we'll just sample my favorites by the creators of the James Bond, 007 books.

Buonaparte Ignace Gallia, or Mr. B.I.G., stands six feet six inches and weighs 20 stones. He was born in Haiti and is half-Negro and half-French. Mr. Big is no ordinary criminal. He is highly intelligent and has a great understanding of Voodoo. In 1943, he was called up for military service. At the close of the war, he disappeared for five years; it was believed that he had gone to Russia. He surfaced in Harlem in 1950 and opened a chain of brothels, with a treasure believed to be that of the pirate Bloody Morgan. Mr. Big began financing Communist activities. He was believed by his followers to be a Zombie and was a most fearsome being.

When Bond first saw him, he noted, "a great football of a head, twice the normal size and very nearly round. The skin was grey-black, taut and shining like the face of a week-old corpse in the river. It was hairless, except for some grey-brown fluff above the ears. There were no eyebrows and no eyelashes and the eyes were extraordinarily far apart so that one could not focus on them both, but only one at a time. Their gaze was very steady and penetrating. When they rested on something they seemed to devour it, to encompass the whole of it. They bulged slightly and the irises were golden round black pupils that were now wide. They were animal eyes,

## Chapter 10: *Rogues, Scamps & No-Good-Nics*

not human, and they seemed to blaze." (*Live and Let Die*, chapter seven).

Compared to this creature, even Dracula would seem as timid as a field mouse.

In reading Bond, we learn that a villain can be more sinister, such is the case of Doctor No. At an early age he had been involved with a Chinese Tong and had become treasurer of the Hip Sings. Doctor No absconded with a million dollars in gold and later, after being captured and having his hands cut off, slipped out of the United States to an island off Jamaica, named Crab Key. Inside of a mountain he built himself sort of an underground paradise and started a profitable business in guano (bird dung). With profits from this business he financed his passion, that of sabotaging American guided missiles.

When 007 first set eyes on Dr. No, he "came slowly out from behind the desk and moved towards them. He seemed to glide rather than take steps. His knees did not dent the matte, gunmetal sheer of his Kimono and no shoes showed below the sweeping hem."

"Bond's first impression was of thinness and erectness and height. Doctor No was at least six inches taller than Bond, but the straight immovable poise of his body made him seem still taller. The head also was elongated and tapered from a round, completely bald skull down to a sharp shin so that the impression was of a reversed raindrop or rather oil drop, for the skin was of a deep almost translucent yellow.

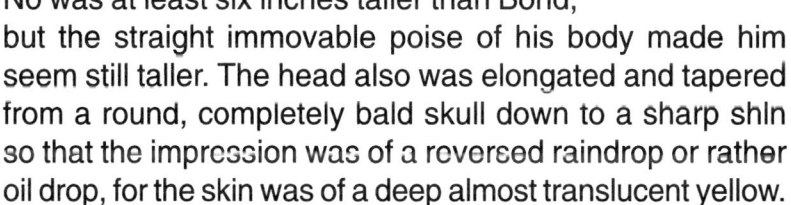

"It was impossible to tell Doctor No's age; as far as Bond could see, there were no lines on the face. It was odd to see a forehead as smooth as the top of the polished skull. Even the cavernous indrawn cheeks below the prominent cheekbones looked as smooth as fine ivory. There was something Dali-esque about the eyebrows, which

## The 007 Dossier

were fine and black and sharply upswept as if they had been painted on as make up for a conjuror. Below them, slanting jet black eyes stared out of the skull. They were without eyelashes. They looked like the mouths of two revolvers, direct and unblinking and totally devoid of expression. The thin fine nose ended very close above a wide compressed wound of a mouth which, despite its almost permanent sketch of a smile, showed only cruelty and authority. The chin was indrawn towards the neck.

"The bizarre, gliding figure looked like a giant venomous worm wrapped in grey tin-foil, and Bond would not have been surprised to see the rest of it trailing slimily along the carpet behind." (*Dr. No*, chapter fourteen).

Ernst Stavro Blofeld is perhaps one of the most enthralling criminals of fiction. He made a total of three appearances in the Bond books, and even in the 1980s, his sinister organization has put in several appearances - in both *For Special Services* and *Role Of Honor*. Blofeld first came to being in *Thunderball,* later in *On Her Majesty's Secret Service* and finally concluded his devious ways in *You Only Live Twice.* Blofeld "was born of a Polish father and Greek mother...," his "eyes were deep black pools surrounded, as Mussolini's were-by very clear whites. Long silken black eyelashes that should have belonged to a woman enhanced the doll-like effect of this unusual symmetry. The gaze of these soft doll's eyes was totally relaxed and rarely held any expression stronger than a mild curiosity in the object of their focus. They converged a restful certitude in their owner and in their analysis of what they observed. To the innocent, they exuded confidence, a wonderful cocoon of confidence in which the observed one could rest and relax, knowing that he was in comfortable, reliable hands. But they stripped the quality or the false and made him feel transparent-as transparent as a fishbowl through whose sides Blofeld examined, with only the most casual curiosity, the few solid fish, the grains of truth,

## Chapter 10: *Rogues, Scamps & No-Good-Nics*

suspended in the void of decent or attempted obscurity. Blofeld's gaze was a microscope, the windows of the world of a superbly clear brain, with a focus that had been sharpened by thirty years of danger, and of keeping just one step ahead of it, and of an inner self-assurance built up on a lifetime of success in whatever he had attempted.

"The skin beneath the eyes that now slowly, mildly, surveyed his colleagues was unpouched. There was no sign of debauchery, illness or old age on the large, white, bland face under the square, wiry black crew-cut. The jaw line, going to the appropriate middle-aged fat of authority, showed decision and independence. Only the mouth, under a heavy, squat nose, marred what might have been the face of a philosopher or a scientist. Proud and thin like a badly healed wound, the compressed, dark lips, capable of only false, ugly smiles, suggested contempt, tyranny and cruelty but to an almost Shakespearean degree. Nothing about Blofeld was small.

## The 007 Dossier

"Blofeld's body weighed about 280 pounds. It had once been all muscle-he had been an amateur weight-lifter in his youth-but in the past ten years it had softened and he had a vast belly that he concealed behind roomy trousers and well-cut double-breasted suits, tailored that evening, out of beige doeskin. Blofeld's hands and feet were long and pointed. They were quick moving when they wanted to be, but normally, as now, they were still and reposed. For the rest, he didn't smoke or drink and he had never been known to sleep with a member of either sex. He didn't even eat very much. So far as vices or physical weaknesses were concerned, Blofeld had always been an enigma to everyone who had known him." (*Thunderball*, chapter five).

(Blofeld might be a nasty character to purchase a used car from.)

These fellows seem a nightmare, but perhaps the most frightening experience to Bond would have been being forced into the ordeal and tribulations of a night of wild recreational kinky lovemaking with Rosa Klebb.

She is described as being neither heterosexual or homosexual, "...a neuter." "She might enjoy the act physically, but the instrument of her enjoyment was of no importance. For her, sex was nothing more than an itch." In *From Russia With Love*, chapter seven, Ian Fleming spends nearly two pages with a description of this, the most horrifying, monstrous, outrageous of the female characters in his books.

"Rosa Klebb would be in her late forties," "...stout, about five foot four, and squat, and her dumpy arms and short neck, and the calves of the thick legs in the drab stocking, were very strong for a woman. The devil knows," "what her breasts were like" and she

## Chapter 10: *Rogues, Scamps & No-Good-Nics*

"...looked like a badly packed sandbag, and in general her figure with its big pear-shaped hips, could only be likened to a 'cello'." She had "...thinning orange hair," tied tight in an "obscene bun," "shiny yellow-brown eyes," a "thickly powdered large-pored nose," a "wet trap of a mouth," "...pale, thick chicken's skin that scagged in little folds under the eyes," "...hard dimpled fists, like knob kerries," and a "...big bundle of bosom." Rosa, we are told, is also unwashed.

No, I don't believe we'll find Bond sniffing around this chick. But all is possible, especially after consuming a half bottle of spirits rated at 65.5 each day or from four to six Vespers.

If starting the series at Book One *Casino Royale* to its present offering, the reader will quickly realize that there is never such a thing as a gentleman's agreement about the rules. Apparently, the text of Rule #1 (to follow all rules) is nonexistent in the dark world of good spy versus bad spy. All's fair in love and war seems to take precedence.

We read of some of the strenuous exercises Bond does each morning to prepare himself for the attempts to kill him. That's kill, as in dead. Dead is an ugly word. No pretend with DEAD.

So Bond does sit-ups, pull-ups, push-ups, leg-ups, some running and hot and cold showers in rehearsal for the ordeals taken from the Fleming books. We'll start with a bomb-blast and move to the car wreck, mangled genitals, an inverted 'M' carved into the right hand, little finger of the left hand broken, barracuda bite, centipede attack, dragged through a coral reef by a boat, injuries from falling off a cliff, another car wreck, a beating, burns from a steam hose, knife-wound to shoulder, kick in head, fight on a train, shot at, poisoning from a kick

## The 007 Dossier

with a knife-shoe, electric burns, more burns from an obstacle course, a fight with a giant squid, knocked out, threatened with a buzz saw, fight with Goldfinger, knocked-out and left on a beach, traction-machine injuries, underwater fight, ski chase, injuries from a bobsled, wife killed, depression, head wound, shot in the shoulder and poisoning from a bullet dipped in cobra vermin. This does not include lists from the Markham, Gardner or Benson books because of the numerous pages it would take to list them all.

    All that just isn't very nice, so let's read about -
    The Swords Of St. Bond
his means to restore some sanity to the world.

## Chapter 11: **The Swords Of St. Bond**

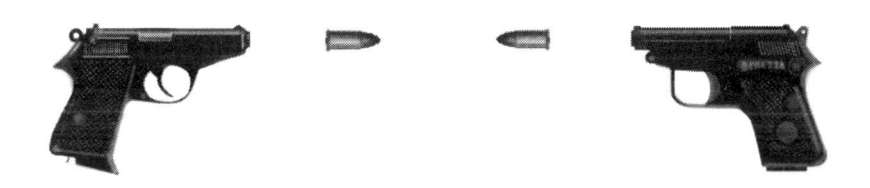

James Bond, this literary myth of the 20th Century, operates in the realm of modern-day demons and dragons. In reading Bond, one quickly learns that the life of a secret service agent is not all perky-breasted, leggy, blue-eyed beauties, fast custom-built Bentleys, Sea Island cotton shirts and chilled bottles of Dom Perignon.

Double 0 seven has a living to earn. From his P.M.S. (Pre-Macho Syndrome) days, we learn something about his schooling. "James Bond had always been a poor student. When he was a boy, he didn't do well in school. It wasn't that he didn't have the capacity to perform well; he was simply bored by it all. A restless soul. Bond was the sort of man who couldn't stay inactive for any length of time. The day-in, day-out routine of school quickly grew tiresome and he needed to move. He was a man of action." (*Tomorrow Never Dies*, chapter four).

He attended both public school and university. "Old school ties" never held much significance for Bond. However he did find an interest in athletics, history and military training. He gained no other proper schooling afterward.

## The 007 Dossier

World War II broke out about that time, and he managed an appointment into the navy as an officer. With education and naval services behind him and the realization that he had an existence to earn, he was inducted into the secret world of MI-6 - the British Secret Service.

From family testament he was granted L1000 a year, and from salary with MI-6 another L1500 a year. After tax, his income was approximately L2000 net. This we learned from *Moonraker*, 1955. We are told he could live very well off this. Double 0 seven is determined to keep the smallest amount possible in his personal bank account, because in his chosen line of work, he knows his time will come - but never when, where or how.

It's near the year 2000 now, and I believe we can assume that his income is much greater now. A guesstimate of L50,000 would not be out of line. Considering deflation of the pound, inflation, cost of living, promotions, civil servant grade rises and whatever is left of the legacy that his Uncle Bruce had left him, I would say that Bond has done rather well for himself. Bond has his flat in London, his full-time housekeeper, the holiday retreat home in Jamaica, a Bentley and the DB5 Aston-Martin, plus surely a very nice wardrobe.

But, 007 has a living to earn, a job to be done, the kind that would put the average Joe Schmoe in a nursing home at least at the conclusion of a fortnight.

For this job he needs the tools of his trade. Bond has destroyed many a Dirty Deed Doers and no-good-nic for King/Queen and country by putting his expertise to work at the proper time for that particular problem. He has been known to fight hand to hand, armed with a sniper's rifle, his prized Beretta and numerous astonishing gadgets from Q-

## Chapter 11: **The Swords Of St. Bond**

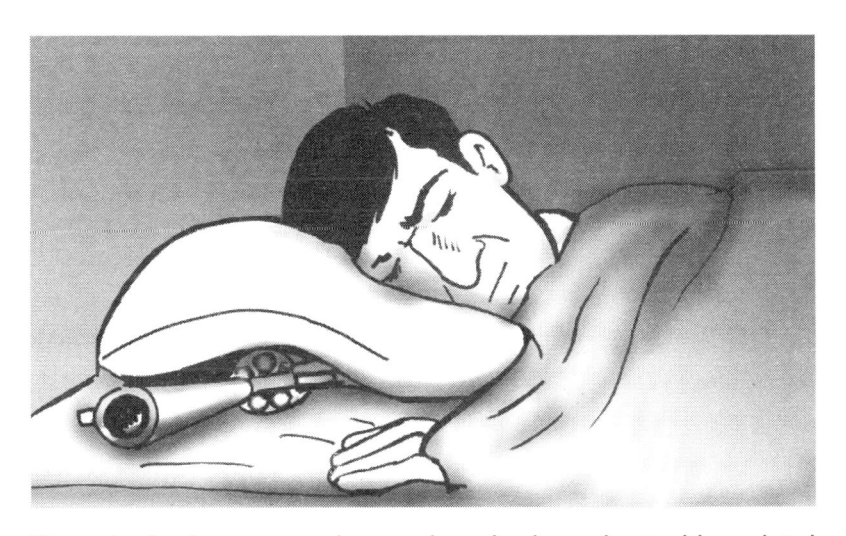

Branch. And on several occasions he has slept with a pistol under his pillow for things that go bang, bump, thump in the night.

Death of the dragon has never given 007 pleasure - or anything to ponder for that matter. For this modern-day St. George, "It was part of his profession to kill people. He had never liked doing it and, when he had to kill, did it as well as he knew how and forgot about it. As a secret agent who held the rare double 0 prefix a license to kill in the Secret Service, it was his duty to be as cool about death as a surgeon was. If it happened, it happened. Regret was unprofessional. Worse, it was a death-watch Beetle in the soul." (*Casino Royale*, chapter eleven).

As stated earlier, James Bond is a highly trained professional killer; he is tough and probably more deadly than any commando and knows more ways to kill than there are symbols in the Chinese alphabet. Double 0 seven can kill with a chop of his hand, with the pressure of his thumb or with a knife. But he is most skilled with a gun. In more than one adventure, Bond visits the basement at Universal Export to the target range, where he spent many an hour sighting and testing the chosen tool of his trade. In *License Renewed* from the pen of John Gardner we learn the

## The 007 Dossier

following about 007's history with firearms:

"During the years when he had made a special reputation for himself in the old Double O Section, Bond had used many hand weapons: ranging from the .25 Beretta - which the Armorer sarcastically dismissed as 'a lady's gun' - to the .38 Colt Police Positive; the Colt .45 automatic; .38 Smith & Wesson Centennial Airweight; and his favorite, the Walther PPK 7.65mm, carried in the famous Berns-Martin triple draw holster.

"By now, however, the PPK had been withdrawn for use, following its nasty habit of jamming at crucial moments. The weapon did this once too often, on the night of March 20, 1974, when a would-be kidnapper with a history of mental illness attempted to abduct Princess Anne and her husband, Captain Mark Phillips. The royal

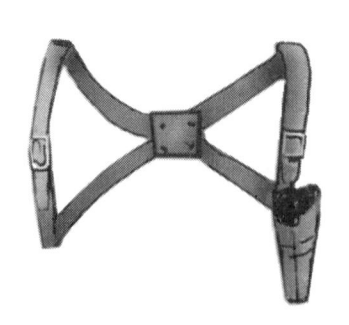

## Chapter 11: *The Swords Of St. Bond*

couple's bodyguard, Inspector James Beaton, was wounded, and, in attempting to return fire, his Walther jammed. That, then, was the end of this particular handgun as far as the British police and security service were concerned.

"Since then, Bond has done most of his range work with either the Colt .45, which was far too heavy and difficult to use in covert field operation, or the old standby .38 Cobra, Colt's long-term favorite snub-nosed revolver for undercover use. Bond, naturally, did not disclose the fact that he carried an unauthorized Ruger Super Blackhawk .44 Magnum in a secret compartment in the Saab.

"Now, minds had to be clear, and decisions taken regarding Bond's field armament, so a lengthy, time-consuming and sometimes caustic battle between Bond and the Armorer concerning the relative merits of weapons.

"They had been through the basic arguments a thousand times already; a revolver is always more reliable than an automatic pistol, simply because there is less to go wrong. The revolver, however, has the double drawback of taking longer to reload usually carrying only six rounds of ammunition in its cylinder. Also, unless you go for the bigger, bulky weapon, muzzle velocity, and therefore, stopping power, is lower.

"The automatic pistol, on the other hand, gives you much easier loading facilities (the quick removal and substitution of a magazine from and into the butt, allows a larger number of rounds per magazine) and has, in the main a more effective stopping power. Yet there is more to go wrong in the way of working parts.

"Eventually it was Bond who had the last word - with a few grumbles from Major Boothroyd - settling on an old, but well tried and true friend, the early Browning 9mm. originally manufactured by Fabrique Nationale-De Guerre in Belgium from Browning patents. In spite of its age, this Browning has accurate stopping power. For Bond, the

## The 007 Dossier

appeal lay in its reliability and size - eight inches overall - and with a barrel length of five inches. A flat, lethal weapon, the early Browning is really a design similar to the .32 Colt and weighs about 32 ounces, having a magazine capacity of seven 9mm. Browning long cartridges, with the facility to carry one extra round in each in the breech.

"Bond was happy with the weapon, knew its limitations, and no hesitation in putting aside thoughts of more exotic handguns of modern manufacture." (*License Renewed*, chapter five).

## Chapter 11: *The Swords Of St. Bond*

Throughout the years, there has been considerable preoccupation with the details which firearms and weapons Bond had used, but no more so than perhaps his choice of a dinner wine or his selection of automobiles. Guns and his knowledge of self-defense and use of them merit more than a brief paragraph in *The 007 Dossier*, because they have played more than a passing installment in Bond's popularity and mystique.

From the pages of Ian Fleming's books, 007 has used the following 33 weapons that I list here, and I may have missed one or two. Keep in mind that some of the really high-tech stuff didn't come along until after that 13-year coma, and near a hundred of these will be listed after the Fleming list.

.38 Colt Police Special
Steel-capped shoes
Limpet mine
Colt .38 Detective Special
Harpoon gun by Champion
Long-barreled .45 Colt Army Special
Nuclear missile
Bofars anti-aircraft gun
Throwing knives by Wilkinson
Cigarette lighter
.25 electric gun (hidden in a copy of
                                          *War and Peace*)
Ordinary chair
.38 Smith & Wesson Centennial Airweight
Steak knife
Spear made of wine-mesh
Bazooka
Daggers concealed in sole of shoe
Bare hands
.45 Colt long barreled
Judo and karate

## The 007 Dossier

Savage 99F rifle
Knife
Turkish steam cabinet
Spear made from broom-handle and knife
Walther PPK
Ski poles
Personal Rolex watch used as knuckle buster
Plastique bombs
Quarter staff
Fists
Cyanide gun
Winchester .308 target gun

And of course that most famous .25 Beretta that was used in Fleming's first five novels. For the remaining Fleming books, the Walther PPK was the principal tool of choice.

In the 20 books since the creator's death on August 12, 1964, 007 has used an encyclopedia of weapons. I am not going to try and list them all. I have listed maybe half from the Markham, Gardner and Benson novels. If you need more (and what for?), you can find them between the pages of the novels.

( If any reader can come up with a total list, we would love to see it. Please send a copy to the publisher for the author. Thank you.)

In no particular order, the list that has been compiled is: knife, Mills grenades, 9mm Browning automatic, a cigarette lighter containing knock-out gas, an antique dueling pistol, tear gas, Ruger Super Blackhawk .44 Magnum, Colt Python .357 Magnum, crossbow, MBA Gyrojet rocket pistol, Sykes-Fairbanks throwing knives, Heckler & Koch VP70 automatic, gasoline bomb, blinding

## Chapter 11: *The Swords Of St. Bond*

aircraft lighter hidden in Saab, Winchester pump gun, Lapp skinning knife, Ruger Redhawk .44 magnum revolver, L2A2 grenade, a walking stick 9mm gun, 9mm ASP automatic with guttersnipe sight, a keycard, a special made Walther PPK that fit the Berns-Martin holster, a scout hidden in the XK-8 Jaguar, a cruise missile, karate, a glass shard, a rough stone, scaffolding, Walther P-99, the heel of shoe, a five-foot eel, AK-47, night vision goggles, choking, plastic dagger, Sea-Vac, homemade bombs, MPSK machine gun, F-14 fighter jet, Harrier jet, MYOAI Marine sniper rifle with long range sight, DC-3 airplane, bow and arrow, Sea Harrier V/STOL (Vertical/Short Take-off and Landing) pronounced "Veestal" aircraft, (we are informed in *Win, Lose or Die* that Commander James Bond R.N.V.R., promoted to Captain for special duty, had always kept his flying hours and instrument rating on both jets and helicopter as a Naval officer for that special assignment that would arise from time to time), kick no-good-nics in ribs (feet), Walther P99, Daewoo .380 automatic pistol, UH-60 Blackhawk helicopter, Stinger missile, 100 mm Cannon ASP 9mm with ferocious Glaser bullets, machine pistol, exploding pen by Q-Branch, magnetic mines, laser watch, 45 mm guns, magnetic grenades, 25 mm anti-aircraft guns, chops and kicks, drowning, Sidewinder missiles, neck snapping, 9mm Browning automatic (from *Win, Lose or Die* we are informed that Bond "...had learned around four hundred ways of killing; four hundred and three if you counted gun, knife

## The 007 Dossier

and strangling rope," chapter nine), Russian Mig 29, Capitol Ejector seat, cell phone by Q-Branch, Heckler & Koch PZK3, gasoline tanker truck, conveyor belt, fire extinguisher, nylon rope, signature gun, C-4 Plastique, Uzi and of course the Russian T-55 tank used in *Goldeneye*.

    Now wimp as I am, I have never shot anything but a rifle, and that was only because I had to in military training in the late 1950s. Most of these weapons that are familiar to Bond are as foreign to me as Eskimo food, and they most likely will remain so. I am pleased that James Bond is on our side - and that he has the knowledge, training, expertise and command of these weapons, and that I am not a no-good-nic in his eyes, because James Bond, 007, R.N.V.R., C.M.G., never ages.

*Chapter 12:* **Chick Charts**

This chapter, "Chick Charts," provides the reader with a concise dossier on each of 34 memorable female characters who have appeared alongside (or in some relation with) our main subject, James Bond 007. The dossier data contained in each "Chick Chart" was obtained from the text of all the Bond books and from the following short stories:

*For Your Eyes Only*
1.) *From A View To A Kill*
2.) *For Your Eyes Only*
3.) *Quantum Of Solace*
4.) *Risico*
5.) *The Hildebrand Rarity*

*Octopussy*
1.) *Octopussy*
2.) *The Living Daylights*
3.) *The Property Of A Lady*

111

*The 007 Dossier*

## CHICK CHART #1

| | |
|---|---|
| Title | *Casino Royale*, 1953/Fleming |
| Girl | Vesper Lynd |
| Hair | Very black, cut square, low on nape of neck |
| Eyes | Deep blue, wide apart |
| Breasts | Fine, splendid ... er ... protuberances |
| Lips and Mouth | Wide and sensual |
| Skin and Makeup | Sun-tanned, trace of makeup |
| Fingernails | Unpainted, cut short |
| Girl's Attire | Medium length of grey soie sarvage, with square cut bodice lasciviously tight across fine breasts. |
| Shoes and Belt: | Square-toed shoes of plain black leather, and a 3-inch hand stitched black belt. |
| Girl's Reaction | "He is rather good looking. He reminds me rather of Hoggy Carmichael, but there is something cold and ruthless in his..." |
| Bond's Reaction | "Bond felt her presence strongly and the prospect of working with her stimulated him. As a woman he wanted to sleep with her, but only after the job was done." |
| Girl's Employer | Double agent - SMERSH and MI-6 |
| Final Remark | Bond: "The Bitch is dead." |

*Chapter 12:* **Chick Charts**

## CHICK CHART #2

| | |
|---|---|
| Title | *Live and Let Die*, 1954/Fleming |
| Girl | Solitaire |
| Hair | Blue-black and fell heavily to her shoulders |
| Eyes | Wide blue eyes |
| Breasts | Hard breasts, each with its stigma of desire |
| Lips and Mouth | Wide, sensual mouth with hint of cruelty |
| Skin and Makeup | Pale, some make-up, and lipstick |
| Fingernails | Short and without enamel |
| Girl's Attire | Long evening dress of heavy mat silk whose classical line was broken by the deep folds which fell from her shoulders and revealed the upper half of her breasts. |
| Shoes and Belt | Not mentioned |
| Girl's Reaction | "She stood just inside the room and stood looking at Bond, taking him in slowly inch by inch, from head to toe." |
| Bond's Reaction | "The message was unmistakable, and an answering warmth must have shown on Bond's cold drawn face." |
| Girl's Employer | Mr. Big |
| Final Remarks | "And you'll have to look after me very well because I shan't be able to make love with only one arm." |

## *The 007 Dossier*

## CHICK CHART #3

| | |
|---|---|
| Title | *Moonraker*, 1955/Fleming |
| Girl | Gala Brand |
| Hair | Dark, brown hair curved inwards at base of neck |
| Eyes | Dark blue |
| Breasts | Splendid; 38-26-38, mole on upper curvature of right breast, pointed hillocks ("Hm!" thought Bond.) |
| Lips and Mouth | Rouge on lips |
| Skin and Makeup | The warmth of her skin was entirely English |
| Fingernails | Square cut with a natural polish |
| Girl's Attire | A rather severe evening dress, was of a charcoal grosgrain with full sleeves that came below the elbow. The wrap-over bodice just showed the swell of her breasts. |
| Shoes and Belt | A wide hand-stitched black leather belt |
| Girl's Reaction | Her eyes looked calmly into his. "How do you do," she said indifferently almost. |
| Bond's Reaction | Beneath her reserve was a very passionate female, he thought. She might know jujitsu, but she also had a mole on her right breast |
| Girl's Employer | Special Branch |
| Final Remark | "I was going to take you off to a farmhouse in France," Bond said. "I was going to see if it's true what they say about the scream of a rose." |

*Chapter 12:* ***Chick Charts***

## CHICK CHART #4

| | |
|---|---|
| Title | *Diamonds Are Forever*, 1956/ Fleming |
| Girl | Tiffany Case |
| Hair | Blond, which fell heavily to her shoulders to catch the light |
| Eyes | Between a light green and a deep gray-blue |
| Breasts | Showed a deep valley between |
| Lips and Mouth | Full and soft and rather sulky; a sinful mouth |
| Skin and Makeup | Lightly tanned and without make up except for a deep red on her lips |
| Fingernails | Short and unpainted |
| Girl's Attire | "She was sitting half-naked" "attired in a black strap bra and tight black lace panties." |
| Shoes and Belt | Black square-toed shoes that looked extremely expensive. |
| Girl's Reaction | She looked at Bond in the mirror, but only briefly and coolly. |
| Bond's Reaction | The sight of the girl "whipped at his senses.' |
| Girl's Employer | The Spangled MOB |
| Final Remark | From Bond - "Get up and walk straight into the bathroom. Get into the tub and lie down." |

*The 007 Dossier*

## CHICK CHART #5

| | |
|---|---|
| Title | *From Russia With Love*, 1957/ Fleming |
| Girl | Tatiana Romonova |
| Hair | Dark brown silken hair, falling heavily to her shoulders |
| Eyes | Wide apart of the deepest blue |
| Breasts | Faultless |
| Lips and Mouth | Lips full and finely stated with a hint of a smile |
| Skin and Makeup | Soft pale with an ivory sheen |
| Fingernails | Not mentioned |
| Girl's Attire | "A quarter inch black velvet ribbon around her neck," "and black silk stockings." |
| Shoes and Belt | Black crocodile shoes with a matching belt (Poor little Russian girl?) |
| Girl's Reaction | There was a squeak of protest from under the sheet, a corner of the sheet was lowered and one large blue eye inspected him. |
| Bond's Reaction | "Well, as a matter of fact, I'm beginning to see some sense to it." |
| Girl's Employer | SMERSH/U.S.S.R. |
| Last Remark | Bond, "I've already got the loveliest...." |

*Chapter 12:* ***Chick Charts***

## CHICK CHART #6

| | |
|---|---|
| Title | *Doctor No*, 1958/Fleming |
| Girl | Honeychile Rider |
| Hair | Ash blond and cut to the shoulder |
| Eyes | Wide apart, deep blue |
| Breasts | Firm and jutted |
| Lips and Mouth | Wide and full |
| Skin and Makeup | A light uniform café au lait with the sheen of dull satin |
| Fingernails | Not mentioned |
| Girl's Attire | Naked except for a broad leather belt with a hunting knife and a green diving mask pushed back on her head |
| Shoes and Belt | Barefoot, broad leather belt |
| Girl's Reaction | Her "hands flew down and across her chest. The muscles of her behind bunched with tension." |
| Bond's Reaction | Bond smiled to himself and took to song. |
| Girl's Employer | Self |
| Final Remark | Bond, "Honey, I can either eat or talk love to you. I can't do both." |

*The 007 Dossier*

## CHICK CHART #7

| | |
|---|---|
| Title | *Goldfinger*, 1959/Fleming |
| Girl | Pussy Galore |
| Hair | Black, worn in untidy urchin cut |
| Eyes | The true deep violet of a pansy |
| Breasts | Hard, with desire |
| Lips and Mouth | Decisive slash of deep vermilion |
| Skin and Makeup | Pale |
| Fingernails | Long silver painted fingernails |
| Girl's Attire | "...a black masculine-cut suit with a high coffee-colored lace jabot |
| Shoes and Belt | Not mentioned |
| Girl's Reaction | "All men are bastards." |
| Bond's Reaction | He felt a sexual challenge all beautiful lesbian women have for men. He thought she was superb. |
| Girl's Employer | Goldfinger by way of SMERSH |
| Final Remark | Bond, "Now." His mouth came ruthlessly down on hers. |

*Chapter 12:* ***Chick Charts***

## SHORT STORY #1     BOOK 8

| | |
|---|---|
| Title | *From A View To A Kill*, 1960/Fleming |
| Girl | Mary Ann Russell |
| Places | Paris and environs |
| Villain | Russian spies |
| Villain Employer | U.S.S.R. |
| Project | To ambush SHAPE dispatch Rider |
| Remarks | Short and well told story |

## SHORT STORY #2     BOOK 8

| | |
|---|---|
| Title | *For Your Eyes Only*, 1960/Fleming |
| Girl | Judy Havelock |
| Places | Jamaica, London, Ottawa, northern Vermont |
| Villain | Von Hammerstein |
| Villain Employer | Self |
| Project | Blackmailing, murdering, etc. |
| Remarks | Good characters, best story |

## SHORT STORY #3     BOOK 8

| | |
|---|---|
| Title | *Quantum of Solace*, 1960/Fleming |
| Girl | None |
| Places | Nassau, Bermuda |
| Villain | None |
| Villain's Employer | None |
| Project | None |
| Remarks | Good reading, full of character |

*The 007 Dossier*

### SHORT STORY #4     BOOK 8

| | |
|---|---|
| Title | *Risico*, 1960/Fleming |
| Girl | Lisl Brown |
| Places | Rome, Venice, environs, Santa Maria |
| Villain | Kristatos |
| Villain's Employer | U.S.S.R. |
| Project | Drug Smuggling |
| Remarks | Too many locations for a short story. Interesting characters. |

### SHORT STORY #5     BOOK 8

| | |
|---|---|
| Title | *The Hildebrand Rarity*, 1960/Fleming |
| Girl | Liz Krest |
| Places | At sea (Indian Ocean) |
| Villain | Milton Krest |
| Villain's Employer | Self |
| Project | Catching rare fish, flogging them to Smithsonian districts, wife beating |
| Remarks | Odd story, Bond's human side shown through |

## Chapter 12: Chick Charts

### CHICK CHART #9

| | |
|---|---|
| Title | *Thunderball*, 1961/Fleming |
| Girl | Domino Vitalis |
| Hair | Blonde, a muddled Brigette Bardot cut |
| Eyes | Dark brown with golden flecks |
| Breasts | High riding, deeply V-ed |
| Lips and Mouth | Proud, sensual, a snarl of desire with a half-pout |
| Skin and Makeup | Sunburn, not overdone |
| Fingernails | Sharp nails |
| Girl's Attire | Pleated cream cotton skirt, almost to the waist. A gondoliers broad-brimmed straw hat with pale blue tails of ribbon and a short sleeved silk shirt of pale blue |
| Shoes and Belt | Flat heeled sandals of white doeskin and a broad white doeskin belt |
| Girl's Reaction | "She decided to go along. But she was not going to make it easy." |
| Bond's Reaction | "...she was the right kind of girl. She might sleep with men but it would be on her own terms." Bond thought he would like to try his strength against hers. |
| Girl's Employer | None |
| Final Remark | Bond's head lie on the pillow, a hand grasped his head and said husklly, "You are to stay here. Do you understand? You are not to go away." |

*The 007 Dossier*

## CHICK CHART #10

| | |
|---|---|
| Title | *The Spy Who Loved Me*, 1962/ Fleming |
| Girl | Vivienne Michel |
| Hair | Dark brown with a natural wave |
| Eyes | Blue, clear, wide with surprise |
| Breasts | Decidedly without a bra |
| Lips and Mouth | Too big which made her look sexy |
| Skin and Makeup | Not mentioned |
| Fingernails | Not mentioned |
| Girl's Attire | Black velvet toreador pants, golden thread Camelot sweater with wide floppy turtleneck sleeves put up to elbow |
| Shoes and Belt | Gold Ferrangano's |
| Girl's Reaction | As she touched Bond's hand, she felt a shock wave down her body and found herself trembling |
| Bond's Reaction | Not mentioned |
| Girl's Employer | Not mentioned |
| Final Remark | "She fitted herself close to his back and thighs." "This is a nice way to sleep - like spoons." |

*Chapter 12:* ***Chick Charts***

## CHICK CHART #11

| | |
|---|---|
| Title | *On Her Majesty: Secret Desires*, 1965/Fleming |
| Girl | Tracy di Vicenzo |
| Hair | Bell of heavy fair hair to her shoulders |
| Eyes | Brilliant blue |
| Breasts | Discreet cleavage, little hills |
| Lips and Mouth | Shocking pink lips |
| Skin and Makeup | Golden tan |
| Fingernails | Not mentioned |
| Girl's Attire | Kind of white dress with V neckline |
| Shoes and Belt | Not mentioned |
| Girl's Reaction | "...shall we go now? I'm not interested in conversation. And you have earned your reward." |
| Bond's Reaction | "Please stay alive, at least for tonight." |
| Girl's Employer | None |
| Final Remark | Bond: "We've got all the time in the world." |

*The 007 Dossier*

## CHICK CHART #12

| | |
|---|---|
| Title | *You Only Live Twice*, 1964/Fleming |
| Girl | Kissy Suzuki |
| Hair | Black with dark brown highlights, heavily waved with a soft fringe |
| Eyes | Almond eyes |
| Breasts | Firm and proud, coarse nippled |
| Lips and Mouth | Petalled |
| Skin and Makeup | A golden sheen of health and vitality |
| Fingernails | Cut very short and broken |
| Girl's Attire | Shawls and blankets, worn with a fronted triangle of black cotton |
| Shoes and Belt | Black cord, feet bare |
| Girl's Reaction | The black triangle between her legs beckoned. She giggled provocatively. "Stop looking at my black cat." |
| Bond's Reaction | He thought there would be nothing more wonderful than to spend the rest of his life with her. |
| Girl's Employer | Japanese Secret Service |
| Final Remark | Bond threw off his kimono. "Kissy, take off your clothes and lie down there. We'll start at page one," Bond said, referring to the Japanese Pillow Book. |

## Chapter 12: *Chick Charts*

CHICK CHART #13

| | |
|---|---|
| Title | *The Man With The Golden Gun*, 1965/Fleming |
| Girl | Mary Goodnight |
| Hair | A golden belle of hair fell to embrace her neck and at times danced angrily (But it was black in *On Her Majesty's Secret Service*.) |
| Eyes | Wide apart blue eyes, direct |
| Breasts | Bosom |
| Lips and Mouth | Full exciting mouth |
| Skin and Makeup | Golden with sunburn, faint trace of makeup |
| Fingernails | Not mentioned |
| Girl's Attire | A one-piece short-skirted frock of pink gin, heavy with bitters and a single sting of pearls and a handbag. |
| Shoes and Belt | Not mentioned |
| Girl's Reaction | "The buttons are down the back.." |
| Bond's Reaction | He was amused by the conscience the girl had awakened in him. |
| Girl's Employer | The British Secret Service |
| Final Remark | "By the way, is your bedroom decorated in pink with white jalousies and do you sleep under a mosquito net?" |

*The Man With The Golden Gun* was published in 1965, Fleming died in 1964 - Estate published.

*The 007 Dossier*

### SHORT STORY    BOOK 14

| | |
|---|---|
| Title | *Octopussy*, 1966 |
| Girl | None |
| Place | Jamaica, flashbacks to Germany |
| Villain | Major Dexter Smythe |
| Villain's Employer | Self |
| Project | Living off Reichsbank gold |
| Remarks | Weak story, more of a morality situation than a M-I-6 problem |

### SHORT STORY    BOOK 14

| | |
|---|---|
| Title | *The Living Daylights* |
| Girl | None |
| Places | London, West Berlin |
| Villain | "Trigger" |
| Villain's Employer | U.S.S.R. |
| Project | To assassinate Western Agent escaping from the U.S.S.R. to West |
| Remarks | Good story, interesting ending |

### SHORT STORY    BOOK 14

| | |
|---|---|
| Title | *The Property of a Lady*, 1966 |
| Girl | None |
| Places | London |
| Villain | Unidentified KGB Director in London |
| Villain's Employer | U.S.S.R. |
| Project | Forcing high bid at auction to pay off a Russian agent |
| Remarks | Soft story, weak ending, lacks mystery |

*Octopussy* was published in 1966, Fleming died in 1964 - Estate published.

*Chapter 12:* **Chick Charts**

## CHICK CHART #15

| | |
|---|---|
| Title | *Colonel Sun*, 1968/Markham |
| Girl | Ariadne Alexandrou |
| Hair | Tobacco blonde |
| Eyes | Light brown |
| Breasts | Deep and yet youthful, swelling firm |
| Lips and Mouth | Firm dry lips |
| Skin and Makeup | Dossical, tints of tan, white, olive and rose |
| Fingernails | Not mentioned |
| Girl's Attire | Low-cut white pique dress, hoop earrings of beaten gold |
| Shoes and Belt | Not mentioned |
| Girl's Reaction | "...as a woman, a woman learnt to recognize on sight the kind of man who knew how to love. Bond was such a man." |
| Bond's Reaction | "Their eyes caught and held at that moment and Bond was certain that she knew his mind, knew it and responded. But she too much be aware that what they both desired must remain a fantasy." |
| Girl's Employer | U.S.S.R. |
| Final Remark | "No." "We're just prisoners. But let's enjoy our captivity when we can." |

*The 007 Dossier*

## CHICK CHART #16

| | |
|---|---|
| Title | *License Renewed*, 1981/Gardner |
| Girl | Lavender Peacock (Dilly) |
| Hair | Blond, falling around her face in a silk smooth sheen |
| Eyes | Smoldering dark eyes |
| Breasts | Firm, impertinent in splendid proportion |
| Lips and Mouth | Striking by the sensuality of her lower lip |
| Skin and Makeup | Reminiscent of Lauren Bacall |
| Fingernails | Not mentioned |
| Girl's Attire | A V-necked, midcalf length dress of a knitted boucle' and a short, sleeveless gilat in white with navy trimmings and hat. Pearl necklace. |
| Shoes and Belt | Not mentioned |
| Girl's Reaction | "Oh yes, please." Lavender appeared to have recovered her poise. |
| Bond's Reaction | If the photo was accurate, a most stunning girl. Bond allowed an almost inaudible low whistle. |
| Girl's Employer | None. |
| Final Remark | "Yes Dilly, you'll see me again soon." |

## Chapter 12: *Chick Charts*

### CHICK CHART #17

| | |
|---|---|
| Title | *For Special Services*, 1982/Gardner |
| Girl | Cedar Lecter |
| Hair | Dark hair cut into a mass of dark curls |
| Eyes | Large brown eyes, showing a tranquillity |
| Breasts | On full display, well proportioned |
| Lips and Mouth | Feminine smile |
| Skin and Makeup | Not mentioned |
| Fingernails | Not mentioned |
| Girl's Attire | Casual denim skirt and shirt |
| Shoes and Belt | Not mentioned |
| Girl's Reaction | Had other ideas. |
| Bond's Reaction | The planned holiday with Cedar was going to be fun, laughter and purely platonic. |
| Girl's Employer | U.S. State Department/C.I.A. |
| Final Remark | "Okay daughter." "Where do you want to go?" |

*The 007 Dossier*

## CHICK CHART #18

| | |
|---|---|
| Title | *Icebreaker*, 1983/Gardner |
| Girl | Paula Vacker |
| Hair | Thick blonde hair, so heavy that it seemed to fall straight back into place |
| Eyes | Large grey flecked |
| Breasts | She pulled at the tie and the robe fell open |
| Lips and Mouth | Lips built for one purpose, a complexion that would put make up firms out of business. |
| Skin and Makeup | Tan, needing no help from a bottle |
| Fingernails | Not mentioned |
| Girl's Attire | White |
| Shoes and Belt | Not mentioned |
| Girl's Reaction | "For you James, I'm always free but never easy." |
| Bond's Reaction | "Are you free tonight?" It would be a dull evening he knew if she were not available. |
| Girl's Employer | S.U.P.O. - Suojelupoliisi - the Protection Police Force. The Finnish Intelligence and Security Agency. |
| Final Remark | "You should never worry about me." |

*Chapter 12:* **Chick Charts**

**CHICK CHART #19**

| | |
|---|---|
| Title | *Role Of Honor*, 1984/Gardner |
| Girl | Persephone Proud (Percy) |
| Hair | Long ash-blonde that just touched the nape of her neck |
| Eyes | Intent light-grey eyes, twinkling |
| Breasts | Small thrusting breasts |
| Lips and Mouth | Full lips |
| Skin and Makeup | Tanned |
| Fingernails | Not mentioned |
| Girl's Attire | A bare shouldered filmy blue dress |
| Shoes and Belt | Not mentioned |
| Girl's Reaction | "Mr. Bond," she said raising her champagne cocktail to his. |
| Bond's Reaction | "Fascinating," thought Bond. |
| Girl's Employer | CIA |
| Final Remark | She nodded, and he leaned across the table to kiss her. "Who knows?" The next morning they rebooked their tickets. |

*The 007 Dossier*

## CHICK CHART #20

| | |
|---|---|
| Title | *Nobody Lives Forever*, 1986/Gardner |
| Girl | Sukie Tempesta |
| Hair | Long tangle of red hair |
| Eyes | Large, brown with violet flecks that could be the undoing of a man |
| Breasts | Full, firm curved breasts |
| Lips and Mouth | Wide mouth |
| Skin and Makeup | Not mentioned |
| Fingernails | Not mentioned |
| Girl's Attire | Calvin Klein jeans and silk Hermes shirt. She looked well judging from her jewelry. |
| Shoes and Belt | Gucci loafers |
| Girl's Reaction | "...her nose wrinkled and her tongue poked out, like a naughty schoolgirl's." |
| Bond's Reaction | Her hand touched his forearm. Bells of warning rang in his head. |
| Girl's Employer | NUB, Norrech Universal Bodyguards |
| Last Remark | "You actually had my stuff moved into your suite, you hussy." |

## Chapter 12: *Chick Charts*

### CHICK CHART #21

| | |
|---|---|
| Title | *No Deals, Mr. Bond*, 1987/Gardner |
| Girl | Ebbie Heritage |
| Hair | Pert, fluffy blond hair |
| Eyes | Wide blue eyes, twinkling |
| Breasts | Fine, obviously unrestrained, which pushed out hard |
| Lips and Mouth | Confident |
| Skin and Makeup | Child of nature, a picture of happiness |
| Fingernails | Not mentioned |
| Girl's Attire | Claret-colored tight silk shirt and a pleated skirt that lifted and flared |
| Shoes and Belt | Not mentioned |
| Girl's Reaction | A flash of static passed between them. |
| Bond's Reaction | Bond sensed desire that he rarely felt when first meeting a female. |
| Girl's Employer | BfV (Bundescant fur Verfossungschutz) West German equivalent of MI-5 |
| Final Remark | Bond, "Your hand is so cool." To which Ebbie answered, "Woman with cool hand has fire under skirt." |

*The 007 Dossier*

## CHICK CHART #22

| | |
|---|---|
| Title | *Scorpius*, 1988/Gardner |
| Girl | Harriet Horner |
| Hair | Black hair, cut fashionably short |
| Eyes | Light grey, humorous |
| Breasts | Slightly large breasts |
| Lips and Mouth | Humorous mouth |
| Skin and Makeup | Not mentioned |
| Girl's Attire | Severe black skirt, white shirt with black ribbon tied around throat. |
| Shoes and Belt | Not mentioned |
| Girl's Reaction | "Oh," with mock pout. "I was hoping you might try." |
| Bond's Reaction | Bond kissed her lightly on the cheek and gave her a consoling squeeze. |
| Girl's Employer | Undercover agent for the United States Internal Revenue Service |
| Final Remark | "Listen Harriet, I've got some interesting items in my briefcase." "Oh, my God," Harriet said pulling Bond closer, "you've enough interesting things here." |

## Chapter 12: *Chick Charts*

### CHICK CHART #23

| | |
|---|---|
| Title | *Win, Lose or Die*, 1989/Gardner |
| Girl | Beatrice Maria da Ricci |
| Hair | Black, bubbly, tight-curled foam of hair |
| Eyes | Dark eyes |
| Breasts | Small, firm, exquisite |
| Lips and Mouth | Wide, smiling mouth |
| Skin and Makeup | Cheeky, a summer sweetness |
| Fingernails | Not mentioned |
| Girl's Attire | Tank-top, cutoffs |
| Shoes and Belt | Not mentioned |
| Girl's Reaction | With a husky voice, she asked, "Would you like to lie down with me, Mr. Bond?" |
| Bond's Reaction | They barely made it to the bedroom. |
| Girl's Employer | Foreign Service |
| Final Remark | "I love you very much," and he realized he meant it. |

## *The 007 Dossier*

### CHICK CHART #24

| | |
|---|---|
| Title | *License To Kill*, 1989/Gardner |
| Girl | Pam Kennedy |
| Hair | Brunette, slicked back |
| Eyes | Dark |
| Breasts | Admirable view |
| Lips and Mouth | Not mentioned |
| Skin and Makeup | Lovely |
| Fingernails | Not mentioned |
| Girl's Attire | Crisp pink suit |
| Shoes and Belt | Not mentioned |
| Girl's Reaction | She "gave him an almost curt, utterly disinterested nod." |
| Bond's Reaction | "...in his constant inquisitive hunt for the secret of women, he was anxious to talk to her.' |
| Girl's Employer | U.S. DEA |
| Final Remark | Pam: "Why don't you wait till you're asked?" Reaching for her again, Bond said "Then ask me." |

## Chapter 12: *Chick Charts*

### CHICK CHART #25

| | |
|---|---|
| Title | *Brokenclaw*, 1990/Gardner |
| Girl | Sue Chi-Ho (Chi-Chi) |
| Hair | Black |
| Eyes | Clean, steady, hazel eyes, a brown and green melding, almond-shaped pleasure |
| Breasts | Gentle, small breasts |
| Lips and Mouth | Laughter lines, askew mouth, brilliant smile |
| Skin and Makeup | Like porcelain |
| Fingernails | Not mentioned |
| Girl's Attire | Faded jeans, a white tee-shirt and a short denim jacket |
| Shoes and Belt | Not mentioned |
| Girl's Reaction | "Okay, but you don't know what you're missing." |
| Bond's Reaction | "You hussy," Bond smiled. "But can I take a raincheck? I have one hell of a headache." |
| Girl's Employer | CIA, provided |
| Final Remark | "No! Absolutely no! No way! Never! Negative and out!" |

*The 007 Dossier*

## CHICK CHART #26

| | |
|---|---|
| Title | *The Man From Barbarosa*, 1992/ Gardner |
| Girl | Nina Bibikova |
| Hair | Dark |
| Eyes | Large black eyes |
| Breasts | Thrusting upward, with deep dark aureoles and erect pink nipples like wild raspberries. They did flatten when she lay on her back. Firm and poised and hardly moved |
| Lips and Mouth | A small crescent scar on the left side of her mouth |
| Skin and Makeup | Dark |
| Fingernails | Long |
| Girl's Attire | A crisp blue dress, not unlike a nurse's uniform |
| Shoes and Belt | Not mentioned |
| Girl's Reaction | Her lips parted in an expression acknowledgment and although she did not speak, the quick sliding of her tongue over her lips conveyed the signal. |
| Bond's Reaction | Unsummoned, Bond's mind screened a picture of Nina's face above his, her lips descending onto his. He was filled with an almost tangible sense of yielding flesh |
| Girl's Employer | CIGN |
| Final Remark | "With permission, sir, I'd like to leave." |

*Chapter 12:* **Chick Charts**

## CHICK CHART #27

| | |
|---|---|
| Title | *Death Is Forever*, 1992/Gardner |
| Girl | Praxi Simeon |
| Hair | Dark hair |
| Eyes | Huge brown eyes with lashes that were a gift from God, not purchased from Estee Lauder. |
| Breasts | Not mentioned |
| Lips and Mouth | Rather thick lips, a silver shimmer when laughing |
| Skin and Makeup | A silver invisible shimmer |
| Fingernails | Not mentioned |
| Girl's Attire | White silk shirt and white slacks beautifully cut |
| Shoes and Belt | Broad snakeskin belt with ornate buckle, matching shoes |
| Girl's Reaction | "Nowadays, you can't be too careful," she whispered as she pressed a small package into Bond's hand. |
| Bond's Reaction | He felt a stirring in his loins, knowing that she offered both lust and companionship. |
| Girl's Employer | SIS |
| Final Remark | He saw Praxi's mouth move and knew she was saying she loved him |

*The 007 Dossier*

## CHICK CHART #28

| | |
|---|---|
| Title | *Never Send Flowers*, 1993/Gardner |
| Girl | Flicka von Grusse |
| Hair | Black, shoulder length, thick silky texture. Right side of fall longer than left |
| Eyes | Wide twinkling green eyes, flirting |
| Breasts | Sexual knockout |
| Lips and Mouth | Glowing mouth |
| Skin and Makeup | Her elegance was the kind rarely seen outside fashion magazines |
| Fingernails | Long, fine fingers |
| Girl's Attire | Only the flimsiest of garments |
| Shoes and Belt | Shoes kicked off, stocking feet |
| Girl's Reaction | "James, there are lots of better views where we're going," she says to Bond who is walking behind her. |
| Bond's Reaction | Their shoulders touched and Bond felt the hint of mutual attraction |
| Girl's Employer | Swiss Intelligence, transferred to British SIS |
| Final Remark | "Please, sir, don't send any flowers." |

## Chapter 12: *Chick Charts*

## CHICK CHART #29

| | |
|---|---|
| Title | *Seafire*, 1994/Gardner |
| Girl | Flicka von Grusse |
| Hair | Black, shoulder length, thick silky texture. Right side of fall longer than left |
| Eyes | Wide twinkling green eyes, flirting |
| Breasts | Sexual knockout |
| Lips and Mouth | Glowing mouth |
| Skin and Makeup | Her elegance was the kind rarely seen outside fashion magazines |
| Fingernails | Long, fine fingers |
| Girl's Attire | Thermal underwear, jeans, black shirt, boots, thick fur coat and fur hat |
| Shoes and Belt | Not mentioned |
| Girl's Reaction | "All I want to do is eat and go to sleep in your arms." |
| Bond's Reaction | Bond and Flicka had lived together since the closure of *Never Send Flowers* |
| Girl's Employer | SIS |
| Final Remark | "Tomorrow and for all time, my darling girl." |

## *The 007 Dossier*

### CHICK CHART #30

| | |
|---|---|
| Title | *Goldeneye*, 1995/Gardner |
| Girl | Natalya Fyodoravana |
| Hair | Dark |
| Eyes | Clear brown eyes |
| Breasts | Braless |
| Lips and Mouth | The taste of sweet fruit |
| Skin and Makeup | Dark with high cheekbones |
| Fingernails | Not mentioned |
| Girl's Attire | A long black skirt and white shirt, covered with a patterned waistcoat |
| Shoes and Belt | Stout leather boots |
| Girl's Reaction | "her body thrust against his." |
| Bond's Reaction | Bond drew her close, leaned over and found her mouth with his. |
| Girl's Employer | Russian Computer Operation |
| Final Remark | "Don't be silly." "There's nobody left to see anything." |

*Chapter 12:* ***Chick Charts***

## CHICK CHART #31

| | |
|---|---|
| Title | *Cold Fall*, 1996/Gardner |
| Girl | Beatrice Maria da Ricci |
| Hair | Light bubble of black curls |
| Eyes | Dark eyes |
| Breasts | Small, firm, exquisite |
| Lips and Mouth | Wide smiling mouth |
| Skin and Makeup | Cheeky, a summer sweetness |
| Fingernails | Not mentioned |
| Girl's Attire | Not mentioned |
| Shoes and Belt | Not mentioned |
| Girl's Reaction | ..kicking the door closed. "You have no idea how happy I am to see you, James." |
| Bond's Reaction | "I've been looking forward to this." |
| Girl's Employer | Foreign Service |
| Final Remark | "Why don't I put her in the bedroom. She's from your past and I don't mind sharing you with her." |

*The 007 Dossier*

## CHICK CHART #32

| | |
|---|---|
| Title | *Tomorrow Never Dies*, 1997/Benson |
| Girl | Wai Lin |
| Hair | Long hair parted in the middle, down to her shoulder blades |
| Eyes | Intelligent, lovely almond colored eyes that could melt a man's heart |
| Breasts | The size of small apples, perfect, firm |
| Lips and Mouth | Small and delicate |
| Skin and Makeup | Striking |
| Fingernails | Not mentioned |
| Girl's Attire | Elegant long silver dress |
| Shoes and Belt | Not mentioned |
| Girl's Reaction | She ducked into a crowd to lose him |
| Bond's Reaction | He sensed something dangerous, he was curious and intrigued |
| Girl's Employer | The Chinese People's External Security Force |
| Final Remark | As Wai Lin wrapped her legs around Bond, she said while unzipping his wet suit, "That's the best news I've heard in a long time.' |

## Chapter 12: *Chick Charts*

### CHICK CHART #33

| | |
|---|---|
| Title | *Zero Minus Ten*, 1997/Benson |
| Girl | Sunni Pei |
| Hair | Black, straight, shoulder-length |
| Eyes | Intelligent, lovely almond colored eyes that could melt a man's heart |
| Breasts | The size of apples, firm and natural, nipples erect |
| Lips and Mouth | Not mentioned |
| Skin and Makeup | Sweet skin, soft and smooth, damp with sweat |
| Fingernails | Not mentioned |
| Girl's Attire | Cheongsam, high heels and a smile |
| Shoes and Belt | Not mentioned |
| Girl's Reaction | She leaned in close and whispered in his ear, "and I'd like to see what's in your pants James." |
| Bond's Reaction | He became sexually aroused |
| Girl's Employer | Chinese Triad |
| Final Remark | "You miss your mother, don't you?" |

*The 007 Dossier*

## CHICK CHART #34

| | |
|---|---|
| Title | *The Facts Of Death*, 1998/Benson |
| Girl | Niki Cassandra Mirakon |
| Hair | Black, worn long |
| Eyes | Brown eyes, thick eyebrows |
| Breasts | Full breasts, perfectly molded into a sweat soaked T-shirt |
| Lips and Mouth | Full lips |
| Skin and Makeup | Mediterranean features, tan skin |
| Fingernails | Not mentioned |
| Girl's Attire | Coveralls and a white T-shirt soaked in sweat |
| Shoes and Belt | Not mentioned |
| Girl's Reaction | She moved closer to him...turned him onto his back and began to massage his broad shoulders. |
| Bond's Reaction | He couldn't help stealing a glance or two. |
| Girl's Employer | NIS - Greek National Intelligence Service |
| Final Remark | "You're one hell of a helicopter pilot..." Whereby Niki answers, "It's just a question of knowing how to get it up." |

## Chapter 13: The Dirty Deed Doers

### Book #1

| | |
|---|---|
| Title | *Casino Royale*, 1953/Fleming |
| Villian | Le Chiffre |
| Villian Employer | SMERSH |
| Project | To win at casino to replace misappropriated SMERSH funds |
| Locations | Royale les Eaux, France and London |
| Villian Demise | Shot and killed by SMERSH agent |

### Book #2

| | |
|---|---|
| Title | *Live And Let Die*, 1954/Fleming |
| Villian | Mr. Big |
| Villian Employer | SMERSH |
| Project | To finance SMERSH operations with pirate booty |
| Locations | London, New York, Florida, Jamaica |
| Villian Demise | Killed by sharks after boat explosion |

## *The 007 Dossier*

### Book #3
| | |
|---|---|
| Title | *Moonraker*, 1955/Fleming |
| Villian | Hugo Drax |
| Villian Employer | U.S.S.R. |
| Project | To destroy London with nuclear rocket |
| Locations | London and Kent |
| Villian Demise | Killed by his own rocket when it fell back to earth and blew his submarine to bits |

### Book #4
| | |
|---|---|
| Title | *Diamonds Are Forever*, 1956/Fleming |
| Villian | Jack Spang |
| Villian Employer | The Syndicate (The Spangled Mob) |
| Project | To smuggle diamonds from Africa to the U.S. |
| Locations | French Guinea, London, New York, Saratoga, Las Vegas and Spectreville, Louisiana |
| Villian Demise | Shot by Bond aboard the train Cannonball |

### Book #5
| | |
|---|---|
| Title | *From Russia With Love*, 1957/Fleming |
| Villian | Rosa Klebb and Red Grant |
| Villian Employer | SMERSH |
| Project | To assassinate Bond |
| Locations | U.S.S.R., London, Istanbul, aboard train The Orient Express and Paris |
| Villian Demise | Grant killed by Bond aboard Orient Express; Klebb taken away in a basket by Leiter of the CIA |

## Chapter 13: The Dirty Deed Doers

### Book #6

| | |
|---|---|
| Title | *Dr. No*, 1958/Fleming |
| Villian | Dr. Julius No |
| Villian Employer | SMERSH |
| Project | To beam misinformation to U.S. missiles |
| Locations | London, Jamaica and Crab Key Island |
| Villian Demise | Buried alive in bird dung |

### Book #7

| | |
|---|---|
| Title | *Goldfinger*, 1959/Fleming |
| Villian | Auric Goldfinger |
| Villian Employer | SMERSH |
| Project | To take control of the gold in Fort Knox |
| Locations | Miami, London, Kent, northern France, New York and Fort Knox |
| Villian Demise | Choked to death by 007 |

### Book #8 - Short Stories

| | |
|---|---|
| Book Title | *For Your Eyes Only*, 1960/Fleming |
| Short Story Title | *From A View To A Kill* |
| Villian | Russian Spy Gang |
| Villian Employer | U.S.S.R. |
| Project | To ambush SHAPE dispatch rider |
| Locations | Paris and environs |
| Story Ending | Hideout is discovered, executioner is shot |

# The 007 Dossier

### Book #8 - Short Stories

| | |
|---|---|
| Book Title | *For Your Eyes Only*, 1960/Fleming |
| Short Story Title | *For Your Eyes Only* |
| Villian | Von Hammerstein |
| Villian Employer | Self |
| Project | Blackmail, murder |
| Locations | Jamaica, London, Ottawa and northern Vermont |
| Story Ending | The death of Gonzales, the cross bow death of Von Hammerstein |

### Book #8 - Short Stories

| | |
|---|---|
| Book Title | *For Your Eyes Only*, 1960/Fleming |
| Short Story Title | *Quantum Of Solace* |
| Villian | Not mentioned |
| Villian Employer | Not mentioned |
| Project | Not mentioned |
| Locations | Nassau, also an anecdote set in Bermuda |
| Story Ending | A memoir recounted to Bond |

### Book #8 - Short Stories

| | |
|---|---|
| Book Title | *For Your Eyes Only*, 1960/Fleming |
| Short Story Title | *Risico* |
| Villian | Kristatos |
| Villian Employer | U.S.S.R. |
| Project | To smuggle drugs |
| Locations | Rome, Venice and environs |
| Story Ending | The warehouse burns, Kristatos dies |

## Chapter 13: **The Dirty Deed Doers**

### Book #8 - Short Stories

| | |
|---|---|
| Book Title | *For Your Eyes Only*, 1960/Fleming |
| Short Story Title | *The Hildebrand Rarity* |
| Villian | Milton Krest |
| Villian Employer | Self employed |
| Project | To catch of rare fish, also wife-beating |
| Locations | Off Chagrin Island (Indian Ocean) |
| Story Ending | Death of Krest |

### Book #9

| | |
|---|---|
| Title | *Thunderball*, 1961/Fleming |
| Villian | Ernst Blofeld, Emilio Largo |
| Villian Employer | SPECTRE |
| Project | To blackmail Western government with threats from stolen nuclear bombs |
| Locations | Sussex, Paris, London and the Bahamas |
| Villian Demise | The killing of Largo by Domino with speargun |

### Book #10

| | |
|---|---|
| Title | *The Spy Who Loved Me*, 1962/Fleming |
| Villian | Horror, Sluggsy |
| Villian Employer | Mr. Sanguinetti |
| Project | To burn down motel for insurance, Vivienne's death a bonus |
| Locations | Adirondack Mountains, flashbacks to London and Toronto |
| Villian Demise | Horror and Sluggsy killed in gunfight with 007, getaway car crashes into the lake |

## *The 007 Dossier*

### Book #11

| | |
|---|---|
| Title | *On Her Majesty's Secret Service*, 1963/Fleming |
| Villian | Ernst Blofeld |
| Villian Employer | SPECTRE |
| Project | To extort money by infecting British crops and livestock with pests |
| Locations | Royale, London, Swiss Alps, M's Quarterdeck and Munich |
| Villian Demise | Escapes in car after the killing of Bond's wife (Tracy) |

### Book #12

| | |
|---|---|
| Title | *You Only Live Twice*, 1964/Fleming |
| Villian | Ernst Blofeld |
| Villian Employer | Self |
| Project | To entice people to commit suicide in his private poisonous garden |
| Locations | London, Tokyo, Kyoto, Fukuoka and Kuro Islands |
| Villian Demise | Swordfight with Blofeld, Bond kills him in hand to hand fight |

### Book #13

| | |
|---|---|
| Title | *The Man With The Golden Gun*, 1965/Fleming |
| Villian | Pistols Scaramanga |
| Villian Employer | Castro and the U.S.S.R. |
| Project | To harm Western interests, especially Caribbean sugar |
| Locations | London and Jamaica |
| Villian Demise | Killed by Bond who shot him five times |

(*The Man With the Golden Gun* was published by the estate after the death of Ian Fleming in 1965.)

## Chapter 13: *The Dirty Deed Doers*

### Book #14 - Short Stories

| | |
|---|---|
| Book Title | *Octopussy*, 1966/Fleming |
| Short Story Title | *Octopussy* |
| Villian | Major Dexter Smythe |
| Villian Employer | Self |
| Project | To living off gold stolen from the Reichsbank |
| Locations | Jamaica, flashbacks to Kaiser Mountains in Germany |
| Villian Demise | Killed from bite of scorpionfish |

### Book #14 - Short Stories

| | |
|---|---|
| Book Title | *Octopussy*, 1966/Fleming |
| Short Story Title | *The Living Daylights* |
| Villian | Trigger |
| Villian Employer | U.S.S.R. |
| Project | To assassinate a Western agent escaping U.S.S.R. to West Berlin |
| Locations | London and West Berlin |
| Villian Demise | Wounded by Bond |

### Book #14 - Short Stories

| | |
|---|---|
| Book Title | *Octopussy*, 1966/Fleming |
| Short Story Title | *The Property Of A Lady* |
| Villian | Resident Director of KGB in London |
| Villian Employer | U.S.S.R. |
| Project | To press auction bids higher to pay off a Russian agent |
| Locations | London |
| Villian Demise | Plan was foiled |

(*Octopussy* was published by the estate in 1966 after Ian Fleming's death.)

## The 007 Dossier

### Book #15
| | |
|---|---|
| Title | *Colonel Sun*, 1968/Markham |
| Villian | Colonel Sun |
| Villian Employer | Red China |
| Project | To sabotage a U.S.S.R. summit conference and let British take the blame |
| Locations | London, Athens and Vrakonist Island (between Turkey and Greece) |
| Villian Demise | Bond pushed a knife into Colonel Sun's heart |

### Book #16
| | |
|---|---|
| Title | *License Renewed*, 1981/Gardner |
| Villian | Anton Murik |
| Villian Employer | Self |
| Project | To blackmail major world powers by causing meltdown in six nuclear power plants |
| Locations | Dublin, London, Scotland, Paris and Perpignan |
| Villian Demise | Double 0 seven shot Murik with a gyro-jet pistol and saw his back disintegrate |

### Book #17
| | |
|---|---|
| Title | *For Special Services*, 1982/Gardner |
| Villian | Nena Blofeld (Blofeld's daughter) |
| Villian Employer | SPECTRE |
| Project | To control Space Wolf Satellites |
| Locations | London; New York; Washington, D.C.; Amarillo, Texas and Cheyenne Mountains, Louisiana |
| Villian Demise | Bond used a chair to knock her through a window; outside she was crushed by pythons |

## Chapter 13: **The Dirty Deed Doers**

### Book #18

| | |
|---|---|
| Title | *Icebreaker* |
| Villian | Konrad von Gloda |
| Villian Employer | National Socialist Action Army |
| Project | To create a "Fourth Reich" with a new Fascist Army |
| Locations | Libya, Finland and the U.S.S.R. |
| Villian Demise | Shot and killed in airport by Bond with his Redhawk Magnum |

### Book #19

| | |
|---|---|
| Title | *Role Of Honor*, 1984/Gardner |
| Villian | Colonel Tamil Rahani |
| Villian Employer | SPECTRE |
| Project | To start nuclear war by disrupting a collective arms control agreement involving Russia, the U.S., Great Britain, France and West Germany |
| Locations | London; Monaco; Monte Carlo; Nun's Cross near Banbury, England and Geneva |
| Villian Demise | Escaped to play the game another day |

### Book #20

| | |
|---|---|
| Title | *Nobody Lives Forever*, 1986/Gardner |
| Villian | Colonel Tamil Rahani |
| Villian Employer | SPECTRE |
| Project | To put a contract out on Bond, which paid ten million Swiss francs to the winner; kidnapping May (Bond's housekeeper) to entice 007 from going to ground |
| Locations | Belgium, France, Tyrolean Alps and Key West Shark Island |
| Villian Demise | Died in burning bed |

## *The 007 Dossier*

### Book #21
| | |
|---|---|
| Title | *No Deals, Mr. Bond*, 1987/Gardner |
| Villian | Kolya Chernov (Blackfriar) and Norman Murray |
| Villian Employer | SMERSH |
| Project | To assassinate Western agents, take revenge on Bond |
| Locations | London, Dublin, Kilkenny, Paris, Hong Kong and Cheung Chan Island |
| Villian Demise | Norman Murray shot in head by 007 with two darts, Kolya Chernov taken into custody |

### Book #22
| | |
|---|---|
| Title | *Scorpius*, 1988/Gardner |
| Villian | Vladimir Scorpius (a.k.a. Father Valentine) |
| Villian Employer | The Society of Meek Ones |
| Project | To disrupt British general election, influence U.S. election by credit card scheme and murder |
| Locations | London; Hereford; Glastonbury; Charlotte, North Carolina and Hilton Head Island, South Carolina |
| Villian Demise | Shot three times (arm, hand, foot) by 007, then fell into marsh filled with deadly water-moccasins |

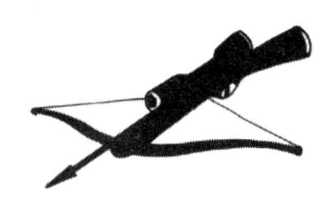

## Chapter 13: **The Dirty Deed Doers**

### Book #23

| | |
|---|---|
| Title | *Win, Lose Or Die*, 1989/Gardner |
| Villian | Bassam Baradj |
| Villian Employer | BAST (Brotherhood of Anarchy and Secret Terror) |
| Project | To abscond with the money and proceeds by the ransom of the HMS Invincible in the BAST Coffers |
| Locations | Straits of Hormuz; London; HMS Invincible; Naples; Bremerhaven, W. Germany; Biscay Bay; Gibraltar |
| Villian Demise | Shot by Beatrice saving Bond |

### Book #24

| | |
|---|---|
| Title | *License To Kill*, 1989/Gardner |
| Villian | Franz Sanchez |
| Villian Employer | Self-employed drug smuggler |
| Project | To continue smuggling drugs |
| Locations | Key West, Florida; Florida environs; Isthmus City; Central America and environs |
| Villian Demise | Consumed by flaming gasoline from tanker truck |

### Book #25

| | |
|---|---|
| Title | *Brokenclaw*, 1990/Gardner |
| Villian | Brokenclaw (Fu-Chu Lee) |
| Villian Employer | Self, with ties to the Republic of China (C.C.I. Central Control of Intelligence and C.E.L.D., Central Liaison Department) |
| Project | Drugs, gambling, local crimes, prostitution and espionage |
| Locations | Victoria, B.C.; London; San Francisco and Northern California |
| Villian Demise | Arrow shot through throat by Bond. |

## *The 007 Dossier*

### Book #26

| | |
|---|---|
| Title | *The Man From Barbarosa*, 1991/Gardner |
| Villian | Boris Stepakov |
| Villian Employer | The Scales of Justice |
| Project | To intensify the war between the coalition and Iraq by dropping a nuclear device on Washington, D.C. |
| Locations | Hawthorne, New Jersey; London; Tampa, Florida; Tel Aviv; Hampshire, England; Moscow; Stockholm; the Ukraine; the Arctic Circle; Bakaj in the Soviet Socialist Republic; Caspian Sea; aboard the Mine Sweeper 252 and Bandan Amzali |
| Villian Demise | Killed himself with a grenade |

### Book #27

| | |
|---|---|
| Title | *Death Is Forever*, 1992/Gardner |
| Villian | Monika Haardt |
| Villian Employer | Wolfgang Weisen, once the head of East Germany's Security Service |
| Project | To destabilize Western Europe |
| Locations | Frankfurt, London, Berlin, Ruhr Valley, Paris, Venice, Calais and Folkestone |
| Villian Demise | Impaled herself on her own knife during knife fight with Bond |

## Chapter 13: *The Dirty Deed Doers*

### Book #28

| | |
|---|---|
| Title | *Never Send Flowers*, 1993/Gardner |
| Villian | David Dragonpol |
| Villian Employer | Self |
| Project | To possess the greatest Museum of Theater, serial assassination and killing |
| Locations | Rome; the Vatican; London; Paris; Washington, D.C.; Langley; Interlaken and Guindewald, Switzerland; Bonn and Andernach, Germany; Milan; Athens and Euro-Disney |
| Villian Demise | Shot in shoulder by Bond, died in flames, which were caused by flare |

### Book #29

| | |
|---|---|
| Title | *Seafire*, 1994/Gardner |
| Villian | Maxwell Tarn |
| Villian Employer | Tarn Enterprises |
| Project | To smuggle weapons for terrorist |
| Locations | St. Thomas, U.S. Virgin Islands; aboard the Caribbean Prince; London; Seville, Spain and Israel |
| Villian Demise | Bond shot him with flare-gun, then he was gunned down by SAS man, died headless |

## The 007 Dossier

### Book #30

| | |
|---|---|
| Title | *Goldeneye*, 1995/Gardner |
| Villian | Alex Trevelyan (006) |
| Villian Employer | Janus Crime Syndicate |
| Project | To use computers for bank robbery |
| Locations | Biv Chemical Processing Plant Number One, far north in the Soviet Empire, Severnaya Station; Arctic Ocean off northern Russia; the south of France; St. Petersburg, Russia; Paris; Miami; Puerto Rico and Cuba |
| Villian Demise | In a fight with Bond, he falls from an antenna dish and is impaled by a spike falling from antenna. |

### Book #31

| | |
|---|---|
| Title | *Cold Fall*, 1996/Gardner |
| Villian | General Brutus Brute Clay (Ice King) |
| Villian Employer | C.O.L.D. (Children of the Last Days) |
| Project | To destroy British Airlines by terrorism, taking control of the U.S. government |
| Locations | London; Washington, D.C.; New York; Dublin; Rome; Pisa; Venice; Puerto Rico and Geneva |
| Villian Demise | Shot by Beatrice, death by drowning |

## Chapter 13: *The Dirty Deed Doers*

### Book #32

| | |
|---|---|
| Title | *Tomorrow Never Dies*, 1997/Benson |
| Villian | Elliot Carver |
| Villian Employer | CMGN (Carver Media Group Network) |
| Project | To control the news before it happens |
| Locations | Khyber Pass (on the border of Afghanistan and Pakistan); London; South China Sea; Oxford, England; Hamburg; Saigon and Okinawa |
| Villian Demise | Chewed to death by the teeth of the Sea-Vac |

### Book #33

| | |
|---|---|
| Title | *Zero Minus Ten*, 1997/Benson |
| Villian | Guy Thackeray |
| Villian Employer | Self (EurAsia Enterprises) |
| Project | To stop the return of Hong Kong to China |
| Locations | Jamaica, England, Hong Kong, Western Australia, London and southern China |
| Villian Demise | Choked to death by Bond in an underwater fight |

*The 007 Dossier*

**Book #34**

| | |
|---|---|
| Title | *The Facts Of Death*, 1998/Benson |
| Villian | Hera Volopoulos |
| Villian Employer | The Number Killer, BioLink Limited, Decada |
| Project | To spread a deadly virus and sell the only cure for billions of dollars, killing millions of people |
| Locations | Los Angeles, Tokyo, Cyprus, the Greek Islands, Texas and England |
| Villian Demise | Bond drowned her at sea and let her body sink to the bottom |

## Chapter 14: *The 007 Trivia Test*

#1 What sits on Bond's desk and never fails to make him smile?
>Answer on page 65.

#2 Who is the mother of his child?
>Answer on page 62.

#3 What is a Vesper?
>Answer on page 44.

#4 What is Bond's mother's maiden name?
>Answer on page 23.

#5 Which no-good-nic releases the roll of newsprint on Bond?
>Answer on page 82.

#6 What is the name of the hamlet where Bond was raised?
>Answer on page 23.

#7 What does the new M think of Bond?
>Answer on page 77.

#8 For whom did James Bond's father work?
>Answer on page 23.

## The 007 Dossier

#9 Who was Bond's live-in tart before he married?
    Answer on page 62.

#10 In what year would 007 have been forced to retire?
    Answer on page 23.

#11 In which book does 007 say that, if he were ever to marry, she would have to be either an airline hostess or Japanese?
    Answer on page 61.

#12 On which side of his face is 007's scar?
    Answer on page 27.

#13 What does Bond nickname his Saab?
    Answer on page 85.

#14 In what year did James Bond start work for MI-6?
    Answer on page 16.

#15 What is the name of the aunt who took Bond in and raised him?
    Answer on page 23.

#16 To which side does James Bond part his hair?
    Answer on page 29.

#17 What is the new M's preferred drink?
    Answer on page 78.

#18 What is James Bond's height and weight?
    Answer on page 27.

#19 What birth date does John Pearson give Bond?
    Answer on page 24.

## Chapter 14: *The 007 Trivia Test*

#20 What does the C.M.G. mean behind 007's name?
    Answer on page 20.

#21 What is the name of Bond's first personal secretary?
    Answer on page 68.

#22 What kind of gun did Bond carry hidden in the Saab?
    Answer on page 105.

#23 In which book does Mary Goodnight end up the Bond Girl?
    Answer on page 69.

#24 What is the full name of Q'ute?
    Answer on page 71.

#25 Who built the super-charger for Bond's 4.5 liter Bentley?
    Answer on page 81.

#26 What is hidden on the back of Bond's hand by plastic surgery?
    Answer on page 27.

#27 How long did Bond keep his first Bentley?
    Answer on page 82.

#28 In what year does 007 receive his C.M.G.?
    Answer on page 20.

#29 What car does 007 turn down for the Aston-Martin DB-3?
    Answer on page 83.

#30 What is Bond's favorite vodka? What is it rated?
    Answer on page 42.

## The 007 Dossier

#31 What is the name of Bond's holiday home in Jamaica?
   Answer on page 38.

#32 In which year does Bond buy his Saab?
   Answer on page 84.

#33 What color are the new M's eyes?
   Answer on page 78.

#34 What languages does James Bond have on file with SMERSH?
   Answer on page 27.

#35 What is the name of the uncle who leaves Bond L250,000?
   Answer on page 85.

#36 What is the best way to serve scrambled eggs?
   Answer on page 49.

#37 From what dealer did he purchase his Bentley in 1984?
   Answer on page 86.

#38 In which book does 007 smoke some 70 cigarettes a day?
   Answer on page 39.

#39 How much money does Bond spend on friends and females after his uncle's will is cleared?
   Answer on page 86.

#40 What does the new M have behind her desk?
   Answer on page 79.

#41 How does Bond prefer to tie his tie?
   Answer on page 33.

## Chapter 14: The 007 Trivia Test

#42 What is Bond's blood pressure at the start of Thunderball?
    Answer on page 41.

#43 In which book does Bond buy the most selfish car in England?
    Answer on page 83.

#44 When dropping pepper in bathtub vodka, what does it remove?
    Answer on page 42.

#45 Who taught 007 to ski?
    Answer on page 22.

#46 What are the two nicknames for the new M?
    Answer on page 76 and 77.

#47 From what kind of chickens does Bond prefer his eggs?
    Answer on page 47.

#48 In which part of London is Bond's flat?
    Answer on page 36.

#49 From what town was Bond's mother?
    Answer on page 23.

#50 How long is Bond's egg boiled by May?
    Answer on page 48.

#51 The Japanese man who Bond kills in the RCA building was on the 36th floor. Where was Bond?
    Answer on page 18.

#52 What is the old M's full name?
    Answer on page 74.

# The 007 Dossier

#53 What is the color of the Bentley that Bond bought in 1984?
> Answer on page 86.

#54 In what year will 007 reach retirement age and be forced to retire to a keeper home in the country?
> Answer on page 25.

#55 From where does the best salmon come, and why?
> Answer on page 51.

#56 Bond said that regret is unprofessional. Worse it is _____ _____ _____ _____ ____.
> Answer on page 103.

#57 How do you say 007 in Cantonese?
> Answer on page 17.

#58 What are the measurements of Mary Goodnight?
> Answer on page 69.

#59 How many rounds does the Browning 9mm hold?
> Answer on page 106.

#60 What color socks does Bond prefer?
> Answer on page 33.

#61 What does SMERSH stand for?
> Answer on page 93.

#62 What kind of holster does Bond use with the Walther PPK?
> Answer on page 104.

#63 From where does Bond's favorite coffee come?
> Answer on page 48.

## Chapter 14: *The 007 Trivia Test*

#64 What is the new M's full name?
Answer on page 78.

#65 What is the name of M's home in Windsor Forest?
Answer on page 74.

#66 How fast can Bond's XK-8 go?
Answer on page 88.

#67 What does 007 sleep in?
Answer on page 34.

#68 How fast did Bond's first Bentley go, and how fast in reserve?
Answer on page 82.

#69 What is the name of Bond's father's old school?
Answer on page 23.

#70 Name five of the unique features that Q Branch has built into 007's XK-8?
Answer on page 89.

#71 What is the name of M's oldest daughter, and what turned Bond off?
Answer on page 75.

#72 When Bond is in England, what is his favorite meal?
Answer on page 47.

#73 How many years does 007 work for the old M?
Answer on page 76.

#74 What would you be offered if you came to M's home?
Answer on page 74.

## The 007 Dossier

#75 What habits does the new M have that are similar to the old M?
>Answer on page 78.

#76 What is the name of the only Bond girl to escape 007's charms?
>Answer on page 59.

#77 What company refined Bond's Saab?
>Answer on page 84.

#78 What kind of watch does Bond wear and what model?
>Answer on page 33.

#79 What surprises Bond about the new M?
>Answer on page 78.

#80 Who is the first maker of Bond's cigarettes? Morlands or Morelands?
>Answer on page 40.

#81 Upon what brand of china does May serve Bond his meals?
>Answer on page 35.

#82 What is "Power" according to Dr. No?
>Answer on page 91.

#83 What do the Double 0s mean to Bond?
>Answer on page 78.

#84 In which book does 007 try to kill the old M?
>Answer on page 74.

## Chapter 14: *The 007 Trivia Test*

#85 Who makes Bond's new cigarettes?
   Answer on page 40.

#86 How long does it take Bond to drive to headquarters?
   Answer on page 37.

#87 What is the compression of his Mark IV Bentley?
   Answer on page 83.

#88 Why did Bond name his new holiday home Jamaica?
   Answer on page 38.

#89 What is Bond privileged to do on active duty?
   Answer on page 28.

#90 On which arm does Bond carry his knife?
   Answer on page 27.

#91 How did James Bond earn his 007 rating?
   Answer on page 17 and 18.

#92 On what mountain do Bond's parents die?
   Answer on page 23.

#93 What does COLD stand for?
   Answer on page 93.

#94 What two events occur in Paris when Bond is 16?
   Answer on page 21.

#95 With whom is 007 in competition for the favors of Mary Goodnight?
   Answer on page 19.

#96 How did James Bond get his name?
   Answer on page 16.

## The 007 Dossier

#97 What is the name of Bond's closest American friend?
   Answer on page 65.

#98 What are Bond's favorite toppings on his toast?
   Answer on page 48.

#99 What type of gun did Bond use when he killed for the first time to earn his 00?
   Answer on page 18.

#100 From the 00 section, with whom does Bond socialize?
   Answer on page 19.

#101 What is the name of the small town in France where Bond has a rendezvous with the waitress, and for what else does he acquire a taste?
   Answer on page 21.

#102 What does SPECTRE stand for?
   Answer on page 93.

#103 Where was Bond's father born?
   Answer on page 23.

#104 What kind of trees line the street where Bond lives?
   Answer on page 36.

#105 In what year does Bond buy his first Bentley?
   Answer on page 81.

#106 How long is the scar on Bond's face?
   Answer on page 29.

#107 In what school does Bond's father enter him when he is born?
   Answer on page 23.

## About The Author

**B.S. "Mac" McReynolds**, renown author of many a junk limerick and poetry, has worked with the media in print, TV and radio. During the 1980s, he managed to escape becoming a professional hostage for both the French and Chinese. Forced into forced labor, he didn't do anything. He has since turned down a consulting position with a comedy channel in Singapore.

Born in Santa Monica, California, Mac has lived in the depressed cities of Newport Beach and Carmel, California. He now lives with many a misguided yuppie on the Monterey Peninsula and La Jolla, California, and does all his research without the aid of a Range Rover or cell phone. Mac is presently working on his next book.

*The 007 Dossier*

# Index

## A

Agent 006 ..................................................19, 94, 160
Alcohol consumption......................................................41
Alexandrou, Ariadne................................................. 127
Amis, Kingsley............................................................. 8
Anherst Villiers...........................................................81
Aquilles Rouges (mountains).........................................23
Aston-Martin DB4GT.................................................. 87

## B

Benson, Raymond...........................7, 8, 54, 56, 59, 67
Bentley cars .....................26, 63, 70, 81 - 84, 86 - 88,
              101, 102, 165, 166, 168, 169, 171, 172
Bentley, Mark II Continental....................................83, 84
Bentley, Mark IV...................................................83, 171
Bentley Mulsanne Turbo...............................................86
Benzedrine...................................................................45
Bibikova, Nina............................................................138
*Birds of the West Indies*..............................................16
Black Hat nightclub.....................................................53
Blades restaurant..............................................42, 45, 92
Blofeld, Ernst....................................................151, 152
Blofeld, Nena.............................................................154
Bond coat of arms......................................................16

175

## The 007 Dossier

Bond, Commander James..................16, 17, 20, 21, 109
Bond, Miss Charmain.......................................................23
Bond's automobiles.........................................................81
Bond's child...................................................................62
Boothroyd, Major................................................84, 88, 105
Brand, Gala.............................................................59, 114
Breakfast, Bond sytle.....................................................47
Brioni clothing................................................................34
Brokenclaw (Fu-Chu Lee)......................................137, 157
Brown, Lisl...................................................................120
Bulletproof glass............................................................85

**C**

C.O.L.D...................................................................93, 160
Canton de Vaud............................................................23
Carver, Elliot...........................................................94, 161
Case, Tiffany..........................................................62, 115
*Casino Royale*........................8, 16, 18, 26, 39, 43,
    44, 47, 50, 59, 62, 66, 81, 82, 99, 103, 112, 147
Castle of Death.............................................................45
CCS (Communication Control System)...................84, 86
Chelsea........................................................................36
Chernov, Kolya........................................................94, 156
CNN..............................................................................77
Coffee, Bond style.........................................................48
*Cold Fall*.......................................................76 - 78, 143, 160
Connery, Sean...............................................................26
Country cottage............................................................37
Crocker, Betty...............................................................61

**D**

da Ricci, Beatrice Maria........................................135, 143
Dalton, Timothy.............................................................27
di Vicenzo, Tracy.........................................54, 62, 69, 123
*Diamonds Are Forever*..........................62, 67, 115, 148
Dossier on James Bond by SMERSH..........................27

176

## Index

Double O status ........ 8, 7, 25, 33, 69, 70, 78, 87, 104
Dr. No ............................. 8, 55, 91, 94 - 96, 149, 170
Dragonpol, David ................................................ 159
Drax, Sir Hugo ..................................................... 92
Dunhill/Ronsun lighter ......................................... 40

### E

Eaton ................................................................... 23
Eggs, scrambled, Bond's recipe ......................... 48
Eye color changes .............................................. 68

### F

Father of James Bond ......................................... 23
Fettes .................................................................. 23
Fifth Sea Lord (Sir Messevy) ................. 42, 68, 74, 76
Firearms list ...................................................... 107
Fleming, Ian ............... 7, 8, 13 -16, 19 - 21, 24, 27, 30,
47, 48, 56, 59, 98, 99, 107, 108, 112 - 116,
118 -120, 122 - 126, 147 - 153
*For Special Services* ................. 40, 67, 71, 96, 129, 154
*For Your Eyes Only* ....................... 61, 111, 149 - 151
*From A View To A Kill* ..................... 21, 81, 111, 119, 149
*From Russia With Love* ................. 7, 20, 27, 29, 50, 55,
67, 98, 116, 148
Fyodoravana, Natalya ...................................... 142

### G

Galore, Pussy ................................................... 118
Gardner, John ................. 8, 24, 27, 29, 56, 59, 67, 68,
100, 103, 108, 128 - 143, 154 - 160
Glenn, John ........................................................ 26
*Goldeneye* .............. 15, 77 - 79, 86, 87, 110, 142, 160
*Goldfinger* ................. 63, 83, 87, 92, 93, 100, 118, 149
Goldfinger, Auric ............................................... 149
Goodnight, Mary ............ 19, 69, 70, 125, 165, 168, 171
GPS navigation ................................................... 89

177

## The 007 Dossier

Grand Corniche ..................................................... 87
Grant, Red .................................................... 92, 94

### H

Haardt, Monika .................................................. 158
Havelock, Judy .................................................. 119
Heritage, Ebbie ................................................. 133
Hermes scarves ................................................... 57
Holiday home in Jamaica ..................................... 37, 87
Hologram headlamps .............................................. 89
Horner, Harriet ................................................ 134
Horror and Sluggsy .......................................... 45, 151
Housekeeper, May ...................... 35 - 38, 47, 62, 79, 155, 167, 170

### I

Ice King ........................................................ 160

### J

Jaguar XJS ....................................................... 87
Jaguar XK-8 Coupe ................................................ 87
Johnson, Paul ..................................................... 8

### K

Kennedy, John F .................................................... 7
Kennedy, Pam .................................................... 136
Kings Road ....................................................... 36
Klebb, Rosa ........................................ 91, 94, 98, 148
Krest, Liz ...................................................... 120
Krest, Milton .............................................. 120, 151
Kristatos ................................................... 120, 150

### L

Lake Geneva .................................................. 21, 81
Largo, Emilio ................................................... 151
Lazenby, George .................................................. 26

178

## Index

Le Chiffre..................................................26, 82, 94, 147
Lecter, Cedar.............................................................129
Leiter, Felix.................................................57, 65, 79, 148
License Renewed..........29, 37, 67, 71, 73, 75, 84, 85,
                                              92, 103, 106, 128, 154
License to Kill.......................................................40, 136
Lin, Wai....................................................................144
Live and Let Die.............................45, 66, 95, 113, 147
Lynd, Vesper........................................................62, 112

**M**

M..............17, 19 - 21, 29, 42, 43, 45, 51, 55, 65 - 68,
70, 73 - 79, 84, 88, 99, 101, 126, 164 - 167, 160, 170
Markham, Robert........................8, 24, 27, 56, 59, 100,
                                                         108, 127, 154
Marksbury, Helena........................................................70
Martini, Bond recipe.....................................................43
Matrimonial possibilities..............................................61
Mawdsley, Barbara......................................................78
May, housekeeper...............................35 - 38, 47, 62,
                                                      79, 155, 167, 170
Messervy, Sir Miles.............................42, 68, 74, 76
MG sports car..............................................................57
Michel, Vivienne..........................................27, 45, 54, 122
Mirakon, Niki Cassandra...............................54, 89, 146
Moneypenny, Miss.........................29, 55, 66 - 68, 172
Moonraker.......24, 43, 45, 51, 59, 69, 82, 102, 114, 148
Moore, Roger...............................................................27
Moreland (Morland) cigarettes.....................................40
Mr. Big (B.I.G.).........................................93, 94, 113, 147
Mulliners......................................................................83
Murcaldy, Laird of.......................................................92
Murik, Anton........................................................94, 154

**N**

Naval Intelligence........................................................15

*The 007 Dossier*

Nelson, Barry..................................................26
New M ..............68, 76 - 79, 164, 166, 167, 169, 170
*New Statesman*..................................................8
Niven, David..................................................26
*No Deal, Mister Bond*..................................................58
No, Dr. Julius..................................................149
*Nobody Lives Forever*..................................68, 132, 155

**O**

Oberhauser, Hannes..................................................22
*Octopussy*..................................................22, 126, 153
Office hours for 007..................................................65
*On Her Majestys Secret Service*...............16, 47, 62, 69, 96, 125, 152
*Once Learned, Twice Tried*..................................................22

**P**

Peacocik, Lavender (Dilly)..................................................128
Pearson, John..................................................24, 164
Pei, Sunni..................................................145
Ponsonby, Loelia..................................................45, 68, 70
Proud, Persephone (Percy)..................................................131

**Q**

Q Branch..................20, 66, 71, 83, 84, 87, 88, 169
*Quantum of Solace*..................................................61, 119
Quarterdeck..................................................74
Q'ute (Anne Reilly)..................................................54, 71, 79, 165

**R**

R.N.V.R..................................................16, 21, 24, 109
Rahani, Col. Tamil..................................................94, 155
RCA Building, Rockefeller Center..................................................17, 167
*Reflections In a Goldeneye*..................................................15
Regents Park..................................................65
*Risico*..................................................111, 120, 150

180

# Index

Role of Honor..................21, 30, 71, 81, 85, 86, 96, 131
Rolex Oyster Perpetual Chronometer............................34
Rolls Royce.................................................................74
Romanova, Tatianna.........................................20, 54
Ronson/Dunhill lighter................................................40
Rothermere, Anne......................................................15
Royal St. George Golf Course...................................65
Russell, Mary Ann....................................................119

## S

Saint Augustine..........................................................63
Sanchez, Franz........................................................157
Scaramanga, Pistols................................................152
Scorpius, Vladimir (Father Valentine)..............134, 156
Scrambled Eggs (Bond's recipe)..............................48
Shamelady................................................................87
Shatterhand, Dr........................................................45
Simeon, Praxi.........................................................139
Simmons, H..............................................................40
SIS Building.............................................................65
Sluggsy and Horror.........................................45, 151
SMERSH.............................27, 29, 54, 91, 93, 147,
                                         149, 156, 166, 168
Smiert Spionam........................................................93
Smoking habit....................................................40, 74
Smythe, Major Dexter......................................126, 153
Solitaire..................................................................113
Spang, Jack............................................................148
Spangled Mob.................................................94, 148
SPECTRE...........................93, 151, 154, 155, 172
St. George and the Dragon..............13, 20, 59, 65, 103
Stepakov, Boris......................................................158
Sun, Colonel.............................74, 84, 94, 127, 154
Sunday Times of London............................................7
Suzuki, Kissy............................................54, 62, 124

181

*The 007 Dossier*

## T

Tanner, Bill...................................................19, 42, 77
Tarn, Maxwell....................................................159
Tempesta, Sukie.................................................132
Thackery, Guy................................................93, 94
The 007 Dossier.........................................9, 26, 107
The Facts of Death....................34, 42, 54, 59, 63, 67,
75, 88, 146, 162
The Hildebrand Rarity..............................111, 120, 151
The Living Daylights.......................................126, 153
The Man From Barbarosa..............................67, 138, 158
The Man With The Golden Gun.................40, 69, 73, 74,
125, 152
The Spy Who Loved Me..............................27, 122, 151
Thunderball..........................41, 67, 83, 96, 98, 151, 167
Tomorrow Never Dies..............67, 78, 87, 101, 144, 161
Transworld Consortium............................................73
Transworld Export Ltd.............................................73
Trevelyan, Alex (Agent 006).....................................160
Trigger..................................................126, 153

## U

Uncle Bruce.......................................................102
Universal Export.............................................73, 103

## V

Vacker, Paula.....................................................130
Vesper (the woman).........................44, 50, 62, 112, 167
Vesper, (the martini)..............................................44
Vickers........................................................23, 24
Virginity, Bond's loss of..........................................21
Volopoulos, Hera.................................................162
von der Drache, Hugo.............................................92
von Gloda, Konrad...............................................155
von Grusse, Flicka..........................................140, 141

*Index*

**W**

*Win, Lose or Die*............................................109, 135, 157
Wolfschmidt vodka........................................................42, 43

**Y**

*You Only Live Twice*.........................16, 28, 45, 49, 56, 75,
96, 124, 152

**Z**

*Zero Minus Ten*........................7, 17, 33, 37, 65, 68, 69,
79, 87, 93, 145, 161

*The 007 Dossier*

## Ordering Form

### Mail - Fax **Ordering Form**

Please send me ____ copies of ***The 007 Dossier***
$23.95 plus $2.05 shipping & handling = **US$26./ book.**
California residents add $1.86 sales tax  =  **US$27.86**

Please send me ____ copies of ***Presidential Blips***
$19.95 plus $2.05 shipping & handling = **US$22. / book.**
California residents add $1.54 sales tax  =  **US$23.54**

My check or money order for $_____ is enclosed.
My Visa/MC credit card # is _____
and the expiration date is (month _____, year _____).
Exact name of card holder _____

Please mail my books to the following:

Name _____

Street Address _____ Apt. # _____

City _____ State ___ ZIP _____

Please mail or fax this Ordering Form with payment to:
**BS** Book Publishing          **Fax (619) 638-1828**
4034 Nobel Drive, #102
University City, CA 92122
Phone (619) 638-0669

*The 007 Dossier*

## Mail - Fax **Ordering Form**

Please send me _____ copies of *The 007 Dossier*
$23.95 plus $2.05 shipping & handling = **US$26./ book.**
California residents add $1.86 sales tax  =  **US$27.86**

Please send me _____ copies of *Presidential Blips*
$19.95 plus $2.05 shipping & handling = **US$22. / book.**
California residents add $1.54 sales tax  =  **US$23.54**

My check or money order for $_____ is enclosed.
My Visa/MC credit card # is _____
and the expiration date is (month _____, year _____).
Exact name of card holder _____.

Please mail my books to the following:

Name _____

Street Address _____ Apt. # _____

City _____ State ___ ZIP _____


Please mail or fax this Ordering Form with payment to:
**BS** Book Publishing          **Fax (619) 638-1828**
4034 Nobel Drive, #102
University City, CA 92122
Phone (619) 638-0669

186

## Ordering Form

### Mail - Fax **Ordering Form**

Please send me ____ copies of ***The 007 Dossier***
$23.95 plus $2.05 shipping & handling = **US$26./ book.**
California residents add $1.86 sales tax   =   **US$27.86**

Please send me ____ copies of ***Presidential Blips***
$19.95 plus $2.05 shipping & handling = **US$22. / book.**
California residents add $1.54 sales tax   =   **US$23.54**

My check or money order for $_____ is enclosed.
My Visa/MC credit card # is _____
and the expiration date is (month _____, year _____).
Exact name of card holder _____.

Please mail my books to the following:

Name _____

Street Address _____ Apt. # _____

City _____ State ___ ZIP _____

Please mail or fax this Ordering Form with payment to:
**BS** Book Publishing          **Fax (619) 638-1828**
4034 Nobel Drive, #102
University City, CA 92122
Phone (619) 638-0669

*The 007 Dossier*

## Mail - Fax **Ordering Form**

Please send me ____ copies of *The 007 Dossier*
$23.95 plus $2.05 shipping & handling = **US$26./ book.**
California residents add $1.86 sales tax  =  **US$27.86**

Please send me ____ copies of *Presidential Blips*
$19.95 plus $2.05 shipping & handling = **US$22. / book.**
California residents add $1.54 sales tax  =  **US$23.54**

My check or money order for $_____ is enclosed.
My Visa/MC credit card # is _____
and the expiration date is (month _____, year _____).
Exact name of card holder _____.

Please mail my books to the following:

Name _____

Street Address _____ Apt. # ____

City _____ State ___ ZIP _____

Please mail or fax this Ordering Form with payment to:
**BS** Book Publishing                **Fax (619) 638-1828**
4034 Nobel Drive, #102
University City, CA 92122
Phone (619) 638-0669

188

# NOTES

# NOTES